TO:EM

Your a great friend!
Thanks

YOUR TIME MY TIME

Have a great graduation,
and good luck next year.

Your friend,
Vanessa
Nelson

Your Time My Time

Ann Walsh

Press Porcépic
Victoria·Toronto

   This edition is published by Porcepic Books Limited, 4252
Commerce Circle, Victoria, British Columbia, V8Z 4M2,
with the assistance of The Canada Council.

Typeset by The Typeworks in Trump 11/13½.
Printed in Canada.

Cover art by Ron Lightburn.

Reprinted 1990, 1991, 1993

Canadian Cataloguing in Publication Data

Walsh, Ann, 1942–
     Your time, my time

     ISBN 0–88878–220–9 (bound). --ISBN
0–88878–219–5 (pbk.)

I. Title.
PS8595.A48Y68 1984   jC813'.54   C84-091069-X
PZ7.W347Yo 1984

For Robin Skelton and Gwen Pharis Ringwood
who taught, encouraged, and had faith.

Chapter 1

Margaret Elizabeth Connell, fifteen years old and sweaty, pushed her hair behind her ears and thought wistfully of air conditioning. The small trailer that she and her mother now called home seemed to absorb the August heat and intensify it until the air felt too hot to breathe.

Elizabeth sighed and looked down at the letter she was writing. Spread out on the arborite top of the kitchen table, the sheet of paper seemed wilted and damp. Her perspiring hands had left dark smudges across the page and it looked as untidy as she felt. She read over what she had just written:

Dear Dad,
    You told me that Wells, British Columbia, population 500 and very historical, would be an interesting place to live for a year. It had a lake nearby to swim in, famous Barkerville just up the road, and all the stores and things that Mom and I would need to keep us busy and happy.
    Dear Dad. You were so wrong! This place is the absolute end of the world! It is hot and dusty, (so dusty that

1

they water down the roads every morning) and dull! There is only one general store and a bunch of tourist places across the highway, and the movie theatre, the Sunset, is only open once in a while. No drugstore. No supermarket. No record store. The Jack of Clubs Lake is close but it's cold (even in this heat!) and has a soggy, muddy bottom. I haven't met anyone my own age yet and I haven't even seen Barkerville in the two weeks we've been here.

Our trailer is small, but it will do for the two of us. It gets awfully hot, though. Also, because it's right behind the hotel, it's really noisy on Friday and Saturday nights when the pub is full. (Should I even bother to tell you that there is only one pub in Wells and the Jack O' Clubs is it?) Late last Friday night someone came staggering around here, looking for his car or something, and threw up right outside the front door. Gross!

Mom is finding that being the cook for the restaurant in the Jack O' Clubs isn't quite the exciting job she thought it would be. She goes to work at noon and is tired and irritable when she gets home at nine.

Oh, Dad, please can I come back to Vancouver and live with you and Brian? I hate it in Wells!

Elizabeth shook her head and slowly began erasing the last paragraph. It wouldn't help her father to know how miserable she was or how unhappy her mother was. Joan Connell had signed a contract to work for a year, and Elizabeth had to stay with her mother in dusty, hot, boring Wells.

She finished erasing and stood up. As she opened the fridge door, reaching for the last can of Coke, her hair swung out against her cheek and stuck to her damp skin. Angrily, she pushed it back behind her ears. Her hair, always straight, seemed more limp than ever in this heat. Her mother and brother, Brian, both had dark black hair that curled slightly, making it easy to handle. Why did she have to get the mousy-red, perfectly straight and often greasy hair that came from her father's side of the family?

To make matters worse, she'd left Vancouver needing a

2

haircut and found, to her dismay, that Wells didn't even have a barber shop, much less a beauty salon. Perhaps her mother would take her into Quesnel on her next day off. Quesnel was about an hour's drive down the highway. It was much larger than Wells and had some decent stores — and beauty salons! Well, if worst came to worst and she couldn't stand it any longer, she'd cut her hair herself!

Back at the table she shoved the letter aside. She'd finish writing to her father this evening when it cooled down a bit. Right now she'd sit and enjoy the cold Coke and try not to think of anything. If she went on with the letter, she knew she'd end up crying, which wouldn't help at all.

A whole year in Wells! And it was all her mother's fault. Her mother, at the age of thirty-six, had decided that she wasn't happy, wasn't being 'fulfilled' by her life in Vancouver. The past year had been miserable. Her parents had fought continually, her mother had cried a great deal, and one week-end her father hadn't come home at all. Then, a month ago, Joan Connell announced that she was moving out for a year, a trial separation before they went ahead with a divorce. She had found the job in the Jack O' Clubs — and she was taking Elizabeth with her.

Elizabeth slammed the empty Coke can down on the table. Her parents had discussed the move and had decided that Elizabeth should go with her mother, like it or not. Elizabeth spent a week trying to change their minds, but they remained firm. "Teen-aged girls need their mothers, especially because fifteen is such a difficult stage." The decision was final.

Great, Elizabeth had thought at the time. *That means there will be two of us going through a difficult time together. Just what we both need!*

She was even more upset when she realized that there was no question of Brian, her twelve year-old brother, going with them. "He *can't* lose a whole year of hockey," her mother had said. "And you know how badly he gets

3

bronchitis, even in Vancouver's mild winters. He couldn't possibly move to such a cold climate. There isn't even a doctor in Wells!"

There wasn't a doctor in Wells — and not much else, either. After only two weeks in the town, Elizabeth began to realize how difficult the year would be. Her mother was busy, working late hours, and she was tired and irritable when she came home. The small trailer was furnished with cheap chrome and plastic furniture; their mattresses were lumpy and stained. Elizabeth missed the big, gracious home in Vancouver, only minutes away from stores, a swimming pool, and movie theatres. She missed her friends, her television programmes (Wells had only one channel), and even her brother, Brian. And she desperately missed her father. More than she had imagined.

Tears began to sting her eyes. *Enough of this, Margaret Elizabeth*, she told herself firmly. *Stop thinking about home. This dumb trailer in this stupid town is your home, at least for a while. There's nothing you can do about it but stick it out and hope that Mom moves back to Vancouver when the year is over. Smarten up, stop worrying, and do something to take your mind off your problems.*

Fine. She *would* do something. Great idea. But what could she do? She carefully listed her options. Go to the hotel and hang around the kitchen, and maybe peel potatoes for dinner? No. Her mother didn't really want her in the kitchen, at least not until she had herself more organized at the new job. Besides, thinking about living in Wells for a year had made her angry at her mother, and her resentment would show. It would be better to stay out of her way.

Perhaps Meg MacDonald could use her to babysit little Fay? (The MacDonalds owned the Jack O' Clubs and Meg worked as assistant manager and bookkeeper.) No. Little Fay was only a year old and would be having her afternoon nap right now.

Well, why not spend some time in the Jack O' Clubs Hotel, exploring and wandering around? The hotel boasted a large lobby with a big fireplace and comfortable old chairs. A steep staircase led out of the lobby to a warren of narrow corridors with surprising twists and turns. There was one place upstairs, a small bay window, that overlooked the flat, marshy grounds behind the hotel. She particularly liked that spot, and would sometimes take a book there and curl up in one of the old leather chairs. It might be cooler than the trailer. Anywhere would be cooler than the trailer!

No. That idea didn't appeal to her today. She didn't really feel like reading.

Okay, then, what about a walk down the street to the Pacific 66? It was an old gas station that sold some gas and oil, but also had the most incredible selection of second-hand 'junk' in Wells. There were old books, shelves of them, and only yesterday she had found a first edition of Ray Bradbury's *Golden Apples of the Sun*. She had been reading nothing but science fiction for a year now, much to her mother's disgust, and the Pacific 66 had a good selection of some of her favourite authors.

Or she could just browse through boxes of kitchen utensils, faded make-up, perfumed soap, candles, souvenirs and gum boots. Perhaps she could find another treasure like the large purple glass ball, an old Japanese fishing float, that she had come across earlier this week. Yes, the Pacific 66 sounded like a good idea — except she didn't have a cent to her name! Until she did some more baby-sitting for the MacDonalds or collected this week's allowance she had better stay away from temptation.

What else was there to do on a hot August afternoon in Wells? She could check out the tiny museum again, spend a few hours among the displays of items saved from the gold-rush days. No, she couldn't do that, either. The museum was closed this afternoon.

Come on, she told herself. *Use the imagination every-*

one says you have! Surely you can think of something better to do than sit around a small, hot trailer. How about a swim!

The thought of the long, hot walk back home took all the pleasure out of that idea.

She looked at her watch. Half-past two. She wouldn't get dinner until seven when the rush was over and all the paying customers in the restaurant had been fed. There were more than four hours to fill in.

Suddenly, she stood up. "Okay," she said aloud. "Hot or not, there is only one thing for you to do this afternoon. Get on your bike, Margaret Elizabeth, and go and discover Barkerville."

Grabbing her baseball cap, the blue one that her father had given her because he said the colour matched her eyes exactly, she stepped out of the trailer and into the hot August sun. Her ten-speed was chained to the back of the trailer. She undid the lock, checked the tires, and swung herself up onto the seat.

She coasted down the hill in front of the hotel, turning left onto the highway. Barkerville was supposed to be about eight kilometers from Wells and, as she looked at the highway unwinding in front of her, the air above it heavy with heat haze, she hoped it wasn't any farther.

Well, Barkerville, she thought as she changed gears and settled down for the long ride, *you better be worth the trip!*

Chapter 2

The trip to Barkerville, although longer than Elizabeth had thought it would be, was enjoyable. The air seemed to get cooler as she rode, and more trees lined the sides of the highway. The marsh, with its winding stream, stretched along beside the road for a long way past Wells, and the hills spread out slowly around her as she cycled.

As she rode into the main parking lot in Barkerville, she noticed that the air was much cooler than in Wells. She must have been climbing more than she had thought. She found a bike stand and chained her bike to it. Then she left the parking lot and headed up the main road towards the historic town.

There was no need to hurry, so she walked slowly, letting the tourists scurry around her clicking their cameras. A sign pointed towards the graveyard; she would check that out on her way back.

Elizabeth was curious about Barkerville. She had heard a great deal about the ghost town that had been restored to look as it had in the days of British Columbia's gold rush.

She walked past the museum, and past a large statue of a miner, perhaps Billy Barker himself, panning for gold. Then she was through the gates and looking down the main street of the town.

Even at first glance, Elizabeth was very impressed with Barkerville: the old wooden buildings with their false fronts weathered to a silvery grey and the long boardwalks above the level of the dirt street. As she stood for a moment and looked down the main street, Elizabeth found herself thinking of western movies. *A gun-slinger should come bursting out of one of the buildings,* she thought. *Then the tourists would huddle to one side and the sheriff would come slowly down the street and a real western gun-fight would take place.*

The hot day had dried out the street and clouds of dust puffed under people's feet, giving the town even more the look of a western movie set.

An old church, tall and weathered, dominated the lower end of the town, its steeple towering well above the rest of the buildings. A sign in front said, Saint Saviour's. Curious, she stepped inside.

The church was empty of tourists for the moment, and the old wooden pews seemed to be silently waiting for a congregation. Elizabeth shivered slightly and hurried outside. The emptiness of the church and the faint smell of dust and mildew had left her with a strange sensation, almost as if she had stepped back in time. It was as if the ghosts of women in bonnets and long skirts, and men in boots and top hats were gathered in the shadows, waiting for her to leave so they could continue their church service.

She shook her head to get rid of the eerie feeling, and, with a shrug, turned her back on the church and started up the main street of Barkerville.

In the next hour Elizabeth discovered Barkerville. She learned a lot about what the town looked like in the old days, and how people lived when it was a booming gold-rush town, but she also learned that there was too much to see, too much to absorb, in one visit.

The houses, furnished and set up as if the occupants were to return any minute, the miners' cabins, the assay office, the drug store, the general store, the hotels and the small Chinatown — too many impressions hit her all at once. After a while she found that she was skipping places. *I'll take a better look next time,* she promised herself. *I'll be back again. Some things will just have to wait until my next visit.*

She stood longest before displays that did not boast a plaster mannequin. The tired looking and somewhat tatty models that stood in many exhibits disturbed the atmosphere that Barkerville itself created. An empty living room with needlepoint lying beside a rocking chair; a kitchen looking as if the cook had just stepped out of the room; a schoolroom with books lying open on old wooden desks — these were the displays that sent peculiar shivers up and down her spine. She felt that if she blinked her eyes, the door would open and the long-dead occupants would come back into the rooms and pick up their needlepoint or school books. It was almost as if *she* were the ghost, standing silently in the doorways and waiting for the people of old Barkerville to go on with their lives.

The crowds of tourists had thinned out now. Elizabeth looked at her watch. It was nearly four. Although she had only spent an hour wandering the main street and hadn't even begun to explore the museum or the mining displays, she felt that she had seen enough for one day. Something was troubling her; a sense of almost losing touch with the real world of 1980.

Perhaps this happens to everyone when they first see Barkerville, she thought. *I'll head home and come back tomorrow. Maybe by then I'll be more prepared for this sense of the past and won't have this funny feeling.*

She decided not to follow the sign that said, To Richfield; it promised a long uphill walk to the old courthouse. Instead, she turned around and started back the way she

9

had come. The Barnard Express wagon, drawn by four sturdy horses, was loading up with a group of tourists. She reminded herself to bring money next time so that she could take the ride. She paused to watch a group of giggling children settle themselves in the carriage and two nervous women perch cautiously on the open benches on top.

A smell of freshly baked bread drifted out from the bakery near the Express Office, and a sign in the window proclaimed, Sourdough Bread, Fresh Daily. Once again regretting her penniless state, she walked past the bakery and headed for the main gate.

Just inside the gate there was a sign announcing that Judge Begbie would be holding court in the Methodist Church at two, three and four o'clock. Checking her watch, she saw that it was just after four. *I wonder if the Judge would mind if I'm a bit late?* she thought. *I'd like to see his performance and it's free! I can sneak in quietly, sit in the back, and no one will notice.*

She hurried to the small church which sat in the shadow of the much larger Saint Saviour's and quietly climbed the wooden stairs. Through a window she caught a glimpse of a black-robed figure towering over the heads of the tourists seated in the pews. She could faintly hear a deep voice, muffled but still loud.

Cautiously she opened the door, eased herself inside and gently shut the door behind her. There was an empty aisle seat two rows in front of her. She was carefully making her way towards it when the actor playing Judge Begbie abruptly stopped speaking and pointed directly at her.

"Young lady," he boomed, "this court has been in session for ten minutes! What is your excuse for interrupting the sworn duties of the Court of Her Majesty the Queen by this unseemly late arrival?"

Everyone in the church turned to stare at her, waiting to see what she would do. Someone giggled.

Elizabeth was suddenly angry. Sure, she was a bit late, but this was just an actor playing a part, not a real judge.

10

He might be wearing a judge's black robes and long horse-hair wig, but he was just an ordinary person and had no right to embarrass her in front of all these people. Her first impulse was to turn around and walk out, but that would be more embarrassing than staying.

No! She gathered her courage, looked the judge straight in the eye and replied, "I'm sorry, Your Honour. The stage from Richfield was unavoidably delayed. I assure you it will not happen again."

The Judge lowered his hand. "Very well, then. I accept your apology. You may take a seat. This court will now resume."

Elizabeth slid into the empty seat and pushed her hair behind her ears. She felt flushed and hot, and the palms of her hands were sweating. She knew she was blushing.

A woman seated beside her smiled appreciatively. "That was good," she whispered. "Are you part of the act?" Elizabeth smiled back and suddenly she didn't feel angry anymore. She had handled herself well, and there was no need to be embarrassed or upset. She gave her attention to the performance, and sat enthralled as The Hanging Judge of the Cariboo told of his life, his reputation and the men he'd helped or hanged over a century ago.

She knew a little bit about the real Judge Begbie. He had been a big man, over six feet five inches tall, with an upswept moustache and a full black beard laced with grey. He had been a stern man, too, with strong opinions and a forceful manner of speaking that would send fear into the hearts of lawbreakers and juries alike. Judge Begbie had almost single-handedly brought law and order to British Columbia.

The actor portraying the Judge resembled him in appearance, even to the dark streak in the centre of his beard. He too was tall; a thin-faced man about fifty years old. He wore no make-up, relying instead on his thick, greying hair and beard, and his neatly trimmed and waxed moustache to help him look the part.

For twenty minutes Elizabeth sat and listened, completely caught up in stories of the life and times of the Judge. The tourists laughed discreetly (this was supposed to be a courtroom after all!) and followed intently as the actor went through his monologue. By the time he finished and was answering questions from the audience, Elizabeth had the feeling that this *was* Judge Begbie, not just some actor playing a part. He had captured the audience, kept them interested and involved in his story, and even in the question period never once lapsed out of the forbidding personality that had been the real Begbie's.

Questions over, the Judge dismissed the court. Applause filled the small church. The Judge allowed it to die down, then leaned across his podium and, pointing a long, slender finger at the audience, announced in a threatening voice, "On this occasion *only* will we permit that outrageous outburst, that applause, in our courtroom. Court dismissed!"

Elizabeth remained seated as the tourists filed past her. Some of them went up to the podium to shake the Judge's hand and offer congratulations.

That was really something! Elizabeth thought. *Why can't all history be that exciting and interesting?*

Then she realized that she and the Judge were alone in the tiny church. He gathered up his law books and started down the aisle towards her. Elizabeth stood, hoping to get out the door before he recognized her as the one who had been so late. But she wasn't fast enough. The Judge stood in the aisle beside her and smiled.

"Hello. You certainly gave me a run for my money when I accused you of being late."

"I'm sorry." Elizabeth felt her face reddening. "I knew I was late, but I did want to see the performance and — "

"Oh, no! Someone is *always* late." The Judge laughed. "I just wish that everyone would answer me as you did, as if I really were Judge Begbie. It helps me to stay in character when the audience co-operates. Thank you."

Somewhat taken aback, Elizabeth smiled shyly.

12

"You're welcome. But I'm still sorry I was late."

"That's okay." The Judge took off his wig and ran his hands through his hair. "This horsehair is unbearably hot in this weather — not to mention these heavy black robes." He smiled at her. "Hey! Haven't I seen you around the Jack O' Clubs Hotel? I had dinner there last week and it seems to me that I saw you."

"Yes. My mother is the new cook."

"Well, you can tell her from me that she certainly is an improvement on the old one. I really enjoyed my meal — which wasn't always the case when you ate at the Jack."

"Thanks," said Elizabeth. "I'll tell her. She's new at cooking, at cooking in a restaurant I mean. She'll be glad to hear the compliment."

The Judge held out his hand. "I'm Evan Ryerson, but most of my friends call me Judge. I guess after five years of doing this part I've begun to think of myself as the Judge as well."

"I'm Elizabeth Connell." She shook hands nervously. Hand shaking was something she didn't do too much of, and she was never sure if you were supposed to give a good hard squeeze or just let your hand sit there.

"Elizabeth?" The Judge looked at her curiously. "Not Liz or Libby or Lizzy or something shorter?"

"No." Elizabeth shook her head. "I've never had a nickname. I've never liked them much. I've always been just Elizabeth or Margaret Elizabeth when someone is mad at me."

"You *are* like an Elizabeth, you know. With that reddish hair and that strong chin you remind me of pictures of a very determined Elizabeth — Elizabeth the First, Queen of England."

Elizabeth blushed again. She seemed to blush at everything these days, and the feeling of her face growing warm added even more to her embarrassment.

"Elizabeth the First was known as Bess when she was younger," the Judge continued. "That's what you look

13

like to me — Bess. You don't mind if I call you Bess, do you? You probably will be an Elizabeth in a few years, but right now you look like a Bess to me."

Elizabeth found that she was strangely flattered by the Judge's nickname for her. "No. I don't mind," she said.

"Well, if you're going to be around here for a while we'll probably be seeing a fair amount of each other. Bess is easier to say than Elizabeth."

"I don't mind," Elizabeth repeated. She thought for a moment. "Bess seems sort of old fashioned, as if it goes with Barkerville and Wells and all the history that's a part of this place. No. I don't mind being called Bess."

"Well then, Bess, you call me Judge if you like. And since we are going to be neighbours (I live in Wells too, you know), then let's be friends."

"All right, Judge." Elizabeth smiled. "By the way, I enjoyed your performance."

"Thanks," the Judge replied. "I enjoy doing it. Judge Begbie was so much a part of the history of the gold rush that I feel honoured to portray him."

They began walking towards the church door. "It made me feel a bit funny," said Elizabeth. "Almost as if you were the real Judge Begbie and this really were Barkerville a century ago."

The Judge opened the door for her. "A lot of people react that way, Bess. What do you think of Barkerville?"

"This was my first trip," said Elizabeth. "I'm not really sure. There is too much to take in at once, and some of the exhibits — well, they almost seemed too real. I felt as if I were a ghost, snooping around people's houses, and that the people themselves might come back at any minute and find me there. I halfway expected to see gunslingers in the main street when I first came through the gate."

"Oh, no!" said the Judge, seriously. "Judge Begbie didn't allow any gun-fighting in Barkerville. It may look like a western town in America, but it was very Canadian, even

14

then. Absolutely no gun-slingers were permitted!"

He looked very stern, almost as if he had been personally responsible for establishing law and order in Barkerville. Then he relaxed. "But I do know what you mean. This town affects me the same way. You know, sometimes I get so involved with Judge Begbie — thinking about him, reading about him, researching stories to use in my monologue — that I feel almost as if I *am* the Judge and that Evan Ryerson is one of those ghosts you talk about. I feel as if I'm just hanging about and peeking in at the Judge's life but that *he* is the real person, not me."

He shook his head. "Fanciful thoughts, aren't they? Listen, let me get rid of this costume and then I'll buy you a Coke at the Wake-Up Jake Café. I could do with something cold to drink. Then we can sit and swap impressions of Barkerville in comfort."

Chapter 3

August 24, 1980

Dear Dad,

If my writing seems a bit funny it's because I'm writing this on my knees as I sit in the cemetery in Barkerville. I have a special place here, under a big old pine tree, out of the way, where the tourists don't often come. There is one lonely grave in this spot, but I can't read what the marker says (except for one big *S* or maybe one of those funny *f's* that they used to make in the old days). The rest of the inscription is weathered and grown over with moss and I haven't got the heart to scrape it away and see what it says.

I like this spot, and I am spending a lot of time here. It is quiet and peaceful. I bring my book and read (or write letters), and sometimes I snooze. Mom is really busy these days and still very tired when she's finished work, so I don't see much of her. She doesn't mind my spending so much time here. It keeps me out of her hair! Somehow this spot isn't spooky at all, in spite of it being in a graveyard. I don't feel nearly as lonely here as I do sitting in the trailer in Wells, so almost every day I get out my bike early in the morning and ride up to Barkerville. Sometimes I go into the town itself, but most of my afternoons are spent right here, under my favourite tree, with a book from the Pacific 66.

I've even memorized some of the headstones. Do you know that there are people here who came from all over the world? It is fascinating to read the epitaphs and wonder what they were like and why they came to Barkerville. The graves are so old that some have full grown trees inside the picket fences that enclose them.

Barkerville is a great place! I think I told you about how it made me feel so peculiar the first day I came here. Well, it still gives me the shivers once in a while, but now that I know it better, that feeling has almost gone away. I spend hours looking at the exhibits and wondering what it would have been like to live here when the town was new.

My favourite display is the Bowron house, built in 1898 by William Bowron, the son of one of the Gold Commissioners. There is a beautiful old piano in the house with one of those mannequins playing it. I don't like the mannequins very much. I've found out that they're made of papier mâché, not plaster as I thought at first, but I still don't like them. The Judge says that six men brought the piano into Barkerville on their backs in the early 1860's for use in one of the saloons!

Anyway, the Bowron house, like all the exhibits, is furnished with antique furniture that fits right in with the age of the town. It has a funny old sideboard with china plates and jugs on it, a clock on the wall that really works, music on the piano stand and an old book lying on a round table in the middle of the room. Then, when you go around to the back of the house, you can see the kitchen with the wood cook stove and the pots and pans and kitchen utensils just sitting there, as if they were waiting for someone to come in and start supper. I really enjoy Barkerville and, as you can see, I'm learning some history as well! I wish you and Brian could come up and visit. I know you'd love it, too.

Well, in case Mom hasn't written to you yet, I guess I'd better tell you that she is sort of worried about me. But she doesn't have to be. She's complaining because I

haven't made any friends yet, and although she says that
Barkerville is a good place for me to spend my time, I
know she thinks that I could find better things to do than
to come here every day. But Dad, there's absolutely nothing to do in Wells! It's not fair, actually. She's the one who
dragged me up here in the first place, and now she's nagging at me for enjoying myself. So, if she does write to
you, don't worry. I have made some friends, good friends,
but they are different from the type of friends I had in Vancouver.

I've told you about the Judge. He is a fantastic person,
and knows a lot of the real history of Barkerville — the
things you can't find in books. He has a daughter who's
married and lives in Nova Scotia, and he brought her up
himself after his wife died, which is one of the reasons, I
guess, he understands me so well. He treats me as if I were
an adult; he never talks down to me the way some teachers do. He's a good listener too, and some days when I get
really lonely he'll let me talk for hours about you and
Brian and Vancouver. I'm glad he's here.

I've also met the members of the acting troupe of the
Theatre Royal. They let me see the show for free if I sit
down front and babysit all the little kids they put there.

The show is a lot of fun. It's a melodrama with music
played on an old piano, and the audience is supposed to
boo the villain and cheer for the hero. They really get carried away sometimes. The whole theatre seems to shake
with the noise. Linda, the girl who plays the heroine, is a
friend of the Judge and she says that when I get older I can
audition for a part in the play. She says that it's hard work
doing two performances a day all summer, but it's a great
experience and you really learn how to act because you
have to keep on doing it, day after day, whether you feel
like it or not. Maybe I'll do that, in a few years.

So, don't worry, Dad. I've got lots of friends. It's just
that they are a bit older than I am. But you always did say
that I was very mature for my age. And when school starts
in a week I know I'll meet some of the other kids and find a
friend my own age. At least, I hope so.

I must go. It's nearly five and I have to head back to
Wells. I am getting enormous leg muscles from all of this

bicycling, but I'm not gaining any weight. Mom has lost a few pounds, too.

I miss you and Brian. Do you think you could find a free week-end to come up and visit? You could have rooms in the Jack O'Clubs Hotel. You wouldn't have to stay with us and move in on Mom's space. I really would like to see you. Please come.

All my love to you and Brian. I do miss you very much.

Love,
Elizabeth
or Bess

(That's what the Judge calls me. He says I look a bit like Queen Elizabeth the First of England and her nickname was 'Bess'. I kind of like it.)

Elizabeth folded the letter carefully and put it away in her backpack. She rubbed her eyes and tucked her hair behind her ears. She really would have to do something about her hair before school started. It was getting so long that it looked scraggly unless she washed it every day.

Getting to her feet, she stretched. Although it would be a long time before it got dark, the days were getting shorter and the shadows lengthened in the graveyard earlier and earlier. There was always a chill in the air in the evenings, no matter how hot the day had been, and lately the early mornings were foggy, hinting of fall.

She shrugged her shoulders into the straps of her backpack and bent to give the old headstone a pat. It was a ritual with her; she gave the anonymous marker a friendly pat whenever she arrived at her favourite spot in the graveyard, and also when she left. As she bent over, her pen fell out of the pocket of her pack and rolled across the grass to the edge of the marker. She knelt to pick it up and as she did, a glint caught her eye. It was just a momentary flash of something shiny in the long grass at the foot of the headstone. She brushed aside the grass and there, half buried in roots and dirt, was a small gold ring.

She picked it up and rubbed away the dirt. It was a small ring, a woman's or a child's. A small red stone was set in the centre, flush with the ring itself, and an intricate pattern of engraving spread from the stone across the top of the ring. Something had been engraved on the inside of it, but the letters were too worn to read.

Well, she thought. *It's my lucky day. I wonder if it's real gold?* She slipped the ring onto the little finger of her left hand. It fit as if it had been made for her.

It's a pretty thing. I guess I should check at the office, though, to see if anyone's reported losing it. I hope no one has. I'd like to keep it.

Idly, she turned the ring around on her finger, wondering about the person it had belonged to and how it had come to be nestled in the grass at the head of an old grave in Barkerville.

Suddenly, her vision blurred. The air around her became hazy, as if a misty curtain had been drawn in front of the trees. She felt weak. Her head ached behind her eyes and, for a moment, she thought that she was going to be sick to her stomach.

She eased herself down onto the grass beside the grave. *I'd better sit down for a while. I must be catching the flu or something.*

Carefully, she put her head between her knees, a trick that she knew was good for getting rid of dizziness. She sat that way for several minutes, then, feeling better, she slowly raised her head.

The wooded graveyard had vanished and in its place was an open field studded with tree stumps and scrub grass. The gravestones which had been so numerous were now thinned to a handful, and her special grave, the one she had been sitting beside, was gone.

Elizabeth blinked her eyes, holding them shut for a few seconds. When she opened them the scene remained the same. Puzzled, and slightly frightened, she got to her feet and made her way to one of the nearest tombstones.

The wooden marker was new, the paint unweathered and the wood unsilvered by time. The grave itself was raised and covered with only a thin growth of grass and weeds, bare earth showing quite clearly in spots. Elizabeth was able to read the epitaph clearly:

IN MEMORY
OF
CHARTRES BREW
BORN AT CORFSIN
COUNTY CLARE, IRELAND
31 OF DEC. 1815
DIED AT RICHFIELD
31 OF MAY, 1870
GOLD COMMISSIONER
AND COUNTY COURT JUDGE

Elizabeth knew the grave and knew of Chartres Brew. He had been a friend of the real Judge Begbie. The presence of a familiar grave reassured her slightly.

The rest of his epitaph had been written by Judge Begbie himself. She had memorized it just last week. Slowly, she read the rest out loud: "A man imperturbable in courage and temper, endowed with a great and varied administrative capacity. A most ready wit, a most pure integrity."

The words were the same. But why was the marker so new looking? Why did the grave look fresh instead of sunken and overgrown the way she had seen it last?

Frightened now, Elizabeth ran from grave to grave, checking for familiar ones. Some markers were weathered, but not badly so. Others seemed recent — one looked as if it had been dug only days ago and was still covered with dried wildflowers. Some graves that should have been there were missing.

She looked for her special place, hoping for more reassurance. The big pine was gone and where it should have been stood a tiny seedling, no more than a foot high. The trees that had shaded the graveyard were also gone and, as she looked around her she realized that both above and below her the hills had been stripped of trees.

Slowly, she sat down and tried to think. What had happened? She had found the ring. Then she'd put it on her finger and. . . . Perhaps if she took it off and started again this nightmare would go away. She pulled the ring from her finger and looked around. Everything remained the same: the bare hills, the smaller, newer-looking graveyard.

Frantically, she shoved the ring back onto her finger. *Stupid thing*, she thought. *Everything was normal until I found it. If I could put it back. . . .* But the grave where she had found the ring was not there, and she had no way of knowing exactly where to put the ring.

Unconsciously, she rubbed her hands together, clenching and twisting them the way her mother did when she was upset. Tears began to smart behind her eyes, and she chewed nervously on her bottom lip. *Take it easy*, she told herself. *You're probably asleep, having a bad dream. You'll wake up soon and stretch and yawn, pick up your backpack and go home.*

She rubbed her hands again, pulling and twisting her fingers. The ring sat comfortably on the little finger of her left hand. She held it with the fingers of her right hand, and in her anxiety began to turn it.

Before the ring had completed one revolution, weakness and nausea gripped her again, and the strange mist gathered and swelled before her. Gasping, she closed her eyes. When the sick feeling had gone, she cautiously opened them again. To her relief, the world was once again the safe, familiar place that she knew. The large pine towered above her once more, her favourite grave was there in its proper place, and the tall trees that sheltered the graveyard whispered softly in the afternoon breeze.

Shakily, Elizabeth got to her feet and made her way to

23

Chartres Brew's grave. The weathered marker leaned slightly to one side, its epitaph worn and hard to read. There was no sign of freshly dug earth and no newly erected grave markers could be seen anywhere in the cemetery.

She took a deep breath and picked up her backpack. Carrying it under one arm she made her way out of the graveyard and down the long winding trail that led to the Barkerville parking lot. She walked faster than she usually did, eager to get away from the graveyard and the frightening experience that she had undergone there.

When she reached her bike she unchained it, then paused for a moment before climbing on and starting home. *Something happened to me,* she thought. *Something very strange happened and I'm not sure what it was. Maybe I fell asleep. Maybe I'm coming down with something. Maybe I was daydreaming again and the dreams just got too real. Anyway, I'm sure it was all in my head and not real at all. And it won't happen again, so I might as well stop worrying about it.*

Feeling a bit better, she put her arms through the straps of her backpack and reached for the handlebars of her bike. Then she saw, snugly encircling the little finger of her left hand, the small gold ring with the red stone.

Chapter 4

Elizabeth reached home later than usual that evening. She took an aspirin, lay down in bed and tried to sleep. But whatever had happened that afternoon in the Barkerville cemetery had left her uneasy, and sleep would not come. She worried about the ring. Should she tell her mother about it? There was no point in trying to tell her mother the rest of what had happened to her today. Joan Connell was a very practical woman and disapproved of anything that, to her, resembled the occult: ghosts, Ouija boards, Tarot cards and science fiction alike. She would not be able to help Elizabeth sort out her feelings about her strange experience in the graveyard.

At nine o'clock, when Joan Connell finished work and returned to the trailer, Elizabeth was still lying in bed. She heard footsteps in the kitchen, then her mother's voice: "Elizabeth? Are you here? What's the matter, dear? You didn't come over for supper."

Elizabeth sighed. "I'm in here, Mom. I just wasn't hungry."

Joan Connell hurried into the bedroom. "You must be sick if you're not hungry," she said. "Here. Let me feel your forehead."

"I'm okay, Mom. I just felt a bit . . . a bit sick to my stomach. So I thought I'd skip dinner and lie down for a while."

"You don't seem to have a fever and you look all right." Joan Connell had finished inspecting her daughter. "Come on, get up, and I'll fix you some warm milk. That will give you some protein at least, and it should help to settle your stomach as well."

Elizabeth groaned inwardly. Her mother was very matter of fact about illness; if you were sick, you were *sick* and stayed right in bed. If you were well, you had no business in bed, so up you got. Make up your mind and be quick about it, was her unstated rule.

"Mom, I really don't want any hot milk." Elizabeth got out of bed and pulled her jeans and teeshirt on.

"Nonsense," her mother replied. "Warm milk is the best thing for you if you aren't feeling well. Besides, you did miss supper." Joan Connell was a short, stocky woman who had fought with her weight all of her life. Her black, curly hair topped a round face with dark eyes, and when she became angry her eyes flashed and she held her chin up. To her, the idea of anyone missing a meal through choice was unbelievable. She battled daily with her own appetite, and often wished that she would not crave food so much. "Were you eating junk food at Barkerville again today? How many Cokes did you have?"

"I didn't have anything today except the lunch I packed. Honestly, Mom, just because you have to count every calorie doesn't mean that I have to, you know. And I'm getting lots of exercise these days."

Elizabeth settled herself at the kitchen table while her mother bustled about preparing the milk and a cup of coffee for herself. Elizabeth hated the taste of warm milk; it reminded her of curdled soup or of cream pies that had gone bad. But, it looked like she would have to drink it this time. "I wrote to Dad today," she said in an attempt to take her mind off the thought of warm milk.

"You're always writing to your father," snapped her mother. "I'm sure he knows more about what you're doing these days than I do."

"Oh, Mom, don't be ridiculous! I always tell you what I've done during the day."

Placing the mug of milk in front of Elizabeth, her mother sat down, holding her own cup of coffee. "Yes. I know what you've been doing during the day, and I want to talk to you about it."

Here it comes, thought Elizabeth.

"You are spending far too much time in Barkerville and I'm not sure I like it."

"But Mom, you said you didn't mind my going up there. You said I was learning some history and it kept me from being bored and I wasn't hanging around here all day and —"

"I know, Margaret Elizabeth. But that was before you started spending all day *every* day up there. You haven't cleaned your room in over a week. Your sheets need changing and there are books and clothes all over the floor. You haven't done any housework, either. I thought that we agreed that, with me working these long hours, you would take over most of the chores."

"Come off it, Mom! It's been too hot to stay in this stupid trailer and do housework. I'll clean my room tomorrow, all right?"

"It's not fair, Elizabeth. You promised —"

"Sure, I promised!" Elizabeth's cheeks flushed in anger. "I promised to try to help you all I could while we were here. But what about me? I have to stay a whole year in this armpit of a town with nothing to do, no one my own age around, and you screaming at me because I spend time in Barkerville, the only place for miles where there's something interesting going on. I know it's not fair. It's not fair to me!"

"Don't shout at me, Elizabeth." Joan Connell's voice was tense. "I'm having a hard enough time as it is, without having to cope with this!"

Elizabeth stood up, pushing away the mug of milk, not caring that it spilled on the table. "If you're having such a hard time why don't we go home!"

They glared at each other for a moment. Then Joan Connell said in a small voice, "Please, Elizabeth."

Elizabeth sat down again, mopping up the spilt milk with a Kleenex. "I'm sorry, Mom," she said at last. "I guess I'm just upset."

Her mother sighed. "I know you are, dear, but we have to stay. You know that your father and I agreed to spend a year apart. We both need time to work things out, and I need time to prove to myself that I can hold down a job, that I can exist outside of the family. I don't want to be just 'Mrs. Connell, Mike's wife' for the rest of my life. I want to be a person in my own right." She took a deep breath, then continued. "You know how important this is to me — to the whole family."

It was Elizabeth's turn to sigh. She'd heard it all before. She knew her mother's reasons for the move, but that didn't make it any easier to live in Wells. "I know, Mom, I know. I'll get busy on the housework tomorrow."

Joan Connell sat beside Elizabeth and put an arm around her. "Try to understand, dear. It isn't easy for me, either. I worry about Brian and your father, and if I'm doing the right thing. I worry about you, too. We've been here nearly a month and you haven't made any friends. You just sit by yourself in the trailer, or wander around Barkerville alone."

"But I do have friends, Mom. The Judge, Linda, and —"

"Elizabeth, you're fifteen years old! You need friends your own age — to listen to music with, talk to, exchange clothes with. You don't do anything that normal girls your age do. You don't even read suitable books! You always have your nose in some science fiction thing, or a horror story."

Elizabeth wanted to shout out, "And whose fault is it that I'm here, away from my friends in Vancouver?" but she choked back the words and attempted a smile instead. "That's not true, Mom. When I read *The Shining* it scared me so badly that I've never read another horror story."

In spite of herself, Joan Connell laughed. "I know that, dear, but you do have a fascination for weird things. First it was that Ouija board, then the Tarot cards and now you're hanging around Barkerville all day — a ghost town. I wonder, sometimes, if you're hoping to see a ghost up there."

Elizabeth smiled. "I don't believe in ghosts, Mom. But something *did* happen..." She stopped, uncertain if she should tell her mother what had happened in the graveyard that afternoon. But Joan Connell was busy with her own thoughts.

"I guess it's just a stage and I suppose that, now that I'm a single parent at least for a year, I worry more about you than I would if your father and I were together. Well, will you try, Elizabeth? Will you try to be happy here?"

"Okay, Mom. I'll try. And I'll bet that you'll find you aren't so tired once you get used to the work. We'll have a good year; wait and see."

Her mother gave her a hug. "Sure we will. Just the two of us. We'll manage." Elizabeth and her mother smiled at each other, the harsh words forgotten, at least for now.

"Listen, Elizabeth. Evan — the Judge — is taking me out tonight. There's a group of people in Wells who paint and do pottery and that sort of thing, and he asked me if I'd like to go over and meet them. Maybe I'll be inspired and get out my old oil paints on my next day off, if I can still remember anything about painting!"

"Sure, Mom. You should go. You need friends your own age, too, you know!"

"Cheeky brat." Her mother grinned at her. "I'm off

then. Pick up your room before you go to bed, okay?"

"Yes, Mom. No problem." Elizabeth paused, then spoke softly. "Mom?"

Her mother turned around, hand on the front door knob. "Yes, dear?"

"Mom? Do you think, when this year is over, that you'll go back to Dad?"

Joan Connell waited a long time before she answered. "I don't know, Elizabeth. It's too early to tell. I need this time away from your father, but it might work out that way. I don't know; I just don't know yet."

"That's okay, Mom. I was just asking."

"I know, Elizabeth. This has been hard on you. Let's both keep our chins up, dear, and hope that things work out. We'll just have to wait and see."

Chapter 5

The next day Elizabeth sat among the tourists that crowded the tiny Wesleyan Methodist Church and waited for the Judge to finish his monologue.

It won't be long now, she thought. The Judge was already telling the story of Cataline, the muleskinner, and how his lands were saved by a timely action of Begbie's.

Elizabeth had decided to talk to the Judge about what had happened to her yesterday. She had stayed awake last night, worried and unable to sleep, long after her mother had returned to the trailer. The Judge had been in Barkerville for a long time. He, if anyone, would be able to help her understand what had happened in the graveyard — if, in fact, anything *had* happened and she wasn't just going crazy.

Staring at the Judge, hoping to catch his eye, she once again had the frightening feeling that the man in the long robes who stood before her was not her friend, Evan, but the real 'Hanging Judge' himself. The Judge finally saw her and acknowledged her presence by nodding to her and saying, "Isn't that a fact, young lady?" after a statement. Elizabeth relaxed.

Come on, Judge, she thought. *Finish talking. I need to tell you about the graveyard.*

As if on cue, the Judge finished his speech, and threw the courtroom open to questions. Luckily, there were only a few, and soon he was bowing to the applause that shook the foundations of the tiny old building. The audience, content with the performance, slowly made its way through the wooden pews and out of the church. The Judge gathered his books and gavel and got ready to leave. As he came down the aisle towards her, he smiled and called a greeting. "Afternoon, Your Majesty. And how's the young Bess today?"

"Fine, Judge. You were great, as usual."

"Thank you." The Judge sat down on the pew beside her. "Are you sure you're fine?" he asked. "You look a bit down-in-the-mouth to me."

"Yes. I'm okay. I was just wondering if...." In spite of herself, Elizabeth felt tears inching their way into her eyes.

"Come on, now." The Judge's voice was firm. "You're not upset because I'm calling you 'Your Majesty' again, are you? You know that's just my little joke; a judge's reverence for a young lady who looks so much like a famous queen." He reached out a hand and patted her on the shoulder. "Come on, now. Don't cry. Just let me take off this wig, then tell me all about it."

Elizabeth grubbed in her pocket for a Kleenex, found a rather sad looking one, and firmly blew her nose, banishing the ready tears. "No. I like your nicknames for me, Judge. It's not that. I guess I need someone to talk to. Can you listen for a while?"

The Judge's moustache, freshly waxed for every performance, now drooped slightly in the heat. He placed his heavy horsehair wig on the pew beside him. Small beads of sweat marked where it had framed his face during the performance, and his cheeks were flushed, but he still looked impressive — tall and dignified and every inch a judge.

"Bess, my dear, I'll listen as long as you want to talk. I know about the disagreement you and your mother had last night."

Suddenly, Elizabeth didn't know how to begin.

"No, it's not that either. It's. . . . "

The Judge sat patiently, waiting for her to start, but the words just wouldn't come. Then, gathering her courage, she began, "Judge, did you ever think that you were going crazy?"

The Judge laughed, a great booming laugh that seemed to come from beyond him, from the boisterous, robust days when Barkerville and Judge Begbie were both young. "You ask an actor that?" he said. "Listen, my young friend, when you act, especially when you act three or four times a day, day after day, when you portray a person who is not yourself, you sometimes get very mixed up. Actors often wonder who they really are.

"You see, the characters sometimes spill over into your real life and you find yourself thinking and behaving like them, rather than like yourself. And when you pretend to be a real person, someone who actually existed, like Judge Begbie, the problem becomes worse.

"I know Judge Begbie so well. I know where he lived, what he read, how he spoke, what he liked to drink — and how much! I know him so thoroughly that sometimes I think he's taken over a part of me. Sometimes I have to stop and say to myself, 'Hey! Did I, Evan, say that, or was it the Judge himself putting words into my mouth?'

"Once in a while I don't even know for sure just who I am. Judge Begbie was such a powerful person that I've had times when I think he's taking over and shoving Evan aside. Often I wonder if. . . . Yes, Bess. Everyone sometimes thinks they're going crazy."

Elizabeth thought she knew her friend fairly well, but

he had just shown her a whole new side of himself. She momentarily forgot her own problem, and just sat and stared at him.

"That wasn't much help, was it?" The Judge smiled. "You ask me to listen to you, and I do all the talking. Well, now that I've had my say, do you want to tell me what's bothering you?"

"It was a help, really Judge. Tell me, do you mean that you can actually see Judge Begbie?"

"No," he replied. "I never quite *see* him, if you mean the way that people see ghosts. But sometimes I'm sure he's here when I do my speech. I can feel a . . . a power, I guess, and my act becomes almost not an act. It's as if I'm the pilot of a plane and suddenly the plane starts flying itself. Once in a while I feel that it isn't *me* up there talking to all those tourists, but him, Judge Begbie himself. It can be a bit frightening."

Elizabeth spoke quickly, afraid that her courage would desert her. "Yesterday, in the graveyard, suddenly everything looked funny. The headstones were new and Chartres Brew's grave was fresh and hadn't grown over and all the trees were gone and. . . . " She stopped, blushed.

Then she recovered and continued more slowly.

"Anyway, I had this funny feeling that it was what the graveyard must have looked like years ago when all the trees were cut down to build houses or for firewood."

She paused, and took a deep breath. "So I thought I'd ask you, and maybe you'd know what happened to me."

The Judge was silent for a moment. "I don't know what to tell you, Bess," he said at last. "This town is so full of memories. The very dust in the streets is rich with the long-gone hopes and fears and dreams of the people who used to live here. Look, Barkerville was re-built to give you just that feeling. You walk down the main street and peer into houses that look as if someone just walked out the door and will return at any moment. An open book lies on the table and you can almost see the woman who left her reading to go into the kitchen and start the stew for dinner.

"That's why we all love Barkerville. Because it's very real, very dramatic. Because the past is here and now. The present and the past overlap to such an extent that we all have a feeling of awe, a sense of history. Maybe your feeling for the past is greater than other people's. Maybe your imagination has been so caught by Barkerville that you subconsciously projected your ideas of what the graveyard looked like long ago, and then thought you saw it."

"But I *did* see it," Elizabeth exclaimed. "I read the grave markers and they were clear and new. There were no trees on the hillside, I'm sure of that."

"Easy, Bess. I didn't say you made it up. I was just trying to give you a logical explanation for what happened. There is another explanation, one that I think is more likely, but it isn't logical and it isn't reasonable."

Elizabeth looked at him. "I think I know," she said. "You're going to say that maybe, somehow, I went back in time to when the graveyard was new. I know. I've thought of that possibility and it frightens me."

"Well, perhaps not really back in time, Bess. Maybe you just caught a very powerful memory from someone or something — a glimpse of what someone long ago, long since dead, had seen. I don't know. I can only make a guess."

Elizabeth gave a short, strained laugh. "I read a lot of science fiction. Maybe it's affected my imagination."

"Perhaps," said the Judge. "And you've just heard my lecture on the impact of Barkerville on people. Barkerville, with its sometimes horrible sense of the past that seems to hang over everything here and to work its way into everyone who stays here for any length of time.

"I don't have a better answer for you, Bess. I wish I had."

"That's all right, Judge. It helped a lot just to be able to

35

talk to you. I don't feel so frightened now. I think I do know what you mean. I love Barkerville, but sometimes it makes me feel strange.

"You said it yourself. It's like history right there over your shoulder, watching you and wanting to be, not *history*, but part of the here and now. It's as if the old times are jealous of the new, and want to come back and be alive again. It scares me, sometimes."

"Bess, my dear, it scares me, too." The judge was serious.

"However, in my judicial wisdom I proclaim that the best cure for the Barkerville blues is a Coke, or maybe one of those new-fangled things called milkshakes, at Wake-Up Jake's. Followed, of course, by a shot of melodrama at Theatre Royal."

"You're right, Judge. And thank you for listening."

"Thank *you*, my dear. I appear to be a more proficient talker than listener, though. But come and speak to me if it happens again, will you? I'm always here, if you need me. And Bess, I'm an expert on the Barkerville blues. A real expert!"

Elizabeth answered him slowly. "Thank you, Judge. I'll remember that. I have a feeling that I'll need someone to talk to before this year is over."

Chapter 6

It was Labour Day, the last day of the frantic tourist season, the last busy, bustling day before the old ghost town settled down for the long, quiet season. Although Barkerville was officially open all year, the number of tourists slowed to a trickle after school started in the fall.

Today the Theatre Royal was giving its final performance before the members of the troupe disbanded and returned to their winter jobs. The Judge would hold court only once more before he, too, carefully took off his robes and packed the horsehair wig away until next summer.

Unlike most of the Theatre Royal's cast and the summer workers who kept Barkerville running smoothly, the Judge had a permanent home in Wells. It was an old miner's cabin that he had insulated, plumbed, and made comfortable. During the winter months he occasionally went to Vancouver or Toronto for an acting job, but he spent most of his time in the small town, working on his cabin and trying, as he somewhat shyly admitted, to write *The Great Canadian Novel*. Elizabeth was glad that the

Judge would be around for most of the winter. She had come to rely a great deal on both his company and his unassuming friendship.

This Labour Day was hot. The long dry spell had held throughout the month of August, bringing happiness to the children and anguish to the fire suppression crews who had fought an unusually large number of fires this year. The tourists bustled down the main street of Barkerville, cameras clicking as they tried to immortalize their final week-end of holiday.

Elizabeth thought that most of the visitors were from the nearby towns of Quesnel, Prince George and Williams Lake. Those from further away would have left for home earlier, not wanting to face a long drive home the day before school started.

The children in the crowd seemed particularly restless, as if they were trying frantically to get every bit of pleasure out of their last day of freedom. Babies cried and grubby faced toddlers clutched stick candy. Their mothers wore looks of patient waiting, as if they were counting the hours until the summer ended, and school and routines began once more.

Today, Barkerville held no charm for Elizabeth. The noise and movement of the crowds made her uneasy. The large numbers of people in front of every exhibit discouraged her. She had been to the Judge's court once today, and did not plan to attend the final show. Afraid that she would get sentimental and perhaps even cry, she was deliberately avoiding the last performance of the season.

Next year, she told herself, settling her baseball cap more firmly on her head. *I'll be able to see it again next year.*

Wishing again that she had arranged to get her hair cut before school started, Elizabeth began to walk slowly through the crowd of tourists, away from the church, where Judge Begbie, for the last time, was calling his court to order.

She had not been to the graveyard since her unusual experience there. Not because she was frightened, she told herself. It just made her feel uncomfortable. However, she still wore the ring that she had found there. No one had responded to the "Found" notices that she had posted, and her mother agreed that she might as well keep it. It fit so well that she hadn't even taken it off since she'd picked it up. By now it was as much a part of her as her unruly hair and blue baseball cap.

Listlessly, she wandered through the crowds, not really paying attention to where she was going, and before she realized it, she found herself on the long shaded trail that led up to the graveyard.

Elizabeth smiled to herself. She had missed the peacefulness of her special spot in the cemetery and had subconsciously headed in that direction. *Well, I might as well go up there,* she thought. *They say that if you fall off a horse the best thing to do is to get right back on and ride. I guess that this is the same sort of thing. I'll go back there, just to prove to myself that, whatever happened, I'm not afraid of it.*

The trail was cool; the tall trees kept it shaded from the sun. Stopping at the gates, she looked at the signpost that told of the first man to be buried on what had once been a part of 'Cariboo' Cameron's claim. Peter Gibson, thirty-one years of age, was buried here on July 24, 1863. He had the first grave in what was originally called the Cameronton Cemetery.

She made her way through the headstones; some marble, but most, like her favourite marker, simply made of a carved slab of wood. A few graves had small wooden fences around them that leaned crazily in one direction or another. Some of the fences were completely missing on one side; still others were intact and stood poised like sentries on guard. Realizing that she was walking on tiptoe and holding her breath, she laughed nervously.

"Margaret Elizabeth," she said to herself, "I do believe

you're frightened after all. Come on, now. Stop being so dumb!"

The secluded corner of the graveyard where she used to spend so much time looked the same as ever. The tall pine tree towered serenely over the grave, shadowing the wooden marker with its obliterated engraving. The long grass underfoot gave way in spots to patches of thick moss that thrived in the acid soil under the evergreen trees. Everything was normal. Everything was quiet and calm.

Dropping her backpack at the foot of the tree, she sat down and leaned against the trunk. She had been foolish to be frightened of this place. There was nothing to be afraid of here. The inhabitants of the old graves slept quietly, the trees rustled gently in the afternoon breeze, and the warm summer odours of earth and grass filled the air. It was a very peaceful spot, and she was sorry now that she had stayed away from it for so long.

She settled herself more comfortably, adjusting her pack so that it formed a cushion against the trunk of the tree. It had been over a week since she'd found the ring and seen, or thought she'd seen, the graveyard as it had been many years ago. Well, she did have a very active imagination. Her parents and teachers had been telling her that for years. Perhaps her imagination had been working overtime that day.

She looked at the ring on her finger. It was a pretty thing, and she was glad that no one had claimed it. One small ray of light found its way through the branches of the trees and caught itself in the red jewel. She turned her hand slowly, watching the ray of sunlight strike a deeper gleam from the red of the stone. *It's almost as if the light is trapped in there*, she thought, and idly turned the ring face down, allowing the shaft of sunlight to free itself.

The sea-sick feeling hit her immediately. Waves of nausea shook her and her head ached. She shut her eyes and groaned, hoping she wouldn't throw up. *Just like the last time*, she thought frantically. *It's happening again.*

40

The sick feeling passed as suddenly as it had come, but Elizabeth didn't open her eyes. *If I don't look it won't be there*, she thought. *But I have to look. I have to find out what's happened.* Slowly, reluctantly, she opened her eyes.

A grey mist swirled around her, clearing slowly. The graveyard was bare of trees. Both the tall pine tree and the grave at her feet had vanished. Again, the number of graves had dwindled, and even from where she sat she could make out the new headstone and raised grave of Chartres Brew. Feeling frightened and helpless, she put her head between her hands and began to cry.

"Where did you come from?" The voice spoke suddenly from behind her. She jumped to her feet and turned around, her heart pounding. A cry that was almost a scream escaped from her throat.

"I'm sorry. I didn't mean to scare you." She was facing a tall young man with longish brown hair and a thick sprinkling of freckles across the bridge of his nose. He wore overalls, stained and well worn, tucked into thick leather work boots. He stared at her as if he couldn't believe she was real. Unable to speak, she stood still and stared back at him, her face showing the fright that the sound of his voice had given her.

"Please don't look at me like that. I won't hurt you. I'm sorry I frightened you, but I didn't see you come up to the graveyard. When I noticed you sitting there I thought. . . ." His voice trailed off. "Please don't keep on looking at me like that. I'm not a spectre. Actually, I thought you were a ghost when I first saw you."

Elizabeth swallowed hard and tried to speak. Her throat was dry and tight and her voice sounded thin. "Who are you?"

"I'm Steven Baker. My Father owns a general store in Barkerville. I haven't seen you before. When did you arrive in town? Who are you?"

"Elizabeth . . . Elizabeth Connell," she managed to reply. Her heart had slowed down now, and she was more in control of herself. "Listen. I have to ask you something. Can you see it?"

"I beg your pardon? See what?"

"The graveyard. The way it looks. All those new graves, and the trees are gone. Do you see it, too?"

Steven looked around. "It looks the same to me as it always has. Is something wrong with it?"

"But Chartres Brew's grave. It's new!"

"Of course. He was buried only in May."

Elizabeth took a deep breath. "He was buried in May of 1870!"

Steven looked at her strangely, then slowly rubbed his hand across the bridge of his nose. Elizabeth could see that it was slightly bent on on the right side, as if it had been broken years earlier and hadn't healed properly. "Of course. He died only three months ago," Steven answered.

She stepped backwards and began rubbing her hands together. "But it's 1980! It's 1980!"

Steven shook his head slowly. "Miss, I don't know why you're so upset or what's frightening you, but I do know that this is September 1, 1870. I'm especially certain of the date because yesterday was my birthday. I just turned seventeen."

"No! You're wrong! It's 1980 and this is Barkerville and I live in Wells and school starts tomorrow and. . . ."

"Wells?" He looked puzzled. "I don't know of the place. Is it far from here?"

Elizabeth's legs suddenly felt weak. She eased herself to the ground and pushed her hair behind her ears. She couldn't think of what to say or what to do. This Steven, if he really were from the year 1870, wouldn't know about Wells—it wasn't built until the 1930s. But how could she sit here and conduct a conversation with someone who lived 110 years ago? This sort of thing only happened in the science fiction books she read, not in real life.

Then the absurdity of the situation struck her. Who

was the ghost — big solid Steven Baker from Barkerville's past, or Margaret Elizabeth Connell from Barkerville's future? Who was having the dream — she or Steven?

She laughed weakly. "Steven Baker, are you really there or am I dreaming you?"

This time Steven backed away. "Excuse me, Miss Elizabeth? I don't understand."

"Listen, Steven. It's not 1870. It's 1980 — at least it was when I came into the graveyard half an hour ago. 1980! Do you understand?"

"No," said Steven. "Miss Elizabeth, you better let me take you home. I think perhaps the sun has been too much for you. Come on, now, I'll help you down the road. Just tell me where you live and I'll get you home to your mother safe and sound."

In spite of herself, in spite of the trembling feeling that hadn't quite left her, Elizabeth began to giggle. "I'm okay, Steven," she said, trying not to let the giggles take over as she thought of what his reaction would be if he could take her home to the modern little trailer in Wells.

"Honestly, I'm not sick and I haven't had too much sun. But one of us is talking to a ghost, and I think it's me!"

"I assure you I'm not a spectre. And I don't see what you find so humorous." He seemed offended. "I still think you're ill. All this talk of 1980. Why, that's not for over a hundred years yet."

Elizabeth became serious again. "That's what I'm trying to tell you, Steven. I am from 1980. Something happened in the graveyard and I found that things had changed and then you appeared. Listen! You're not just playing a joke on me are you? You're not just pretending to be from the past—"

"Practical jokes are cruel and I don't care for them."

"Well then, you must really be from 1870!"

Steven rubbed his nose. "Of course I am. And you are, too."

"No I'm not!" Elizabeth said desperately. "I really am

43

from the future and I only hope I can get back there."

Steven looked her up and down slowly, taking in the faded bluejeans, the old T-shirt and baseball cap. "Well, you *are* dressed differently, more like a boy than a girl." He shook his head. "No. I don't believe it. That's like one of those stories that the French author, Jules Verne, writes. Please, Elizabeth. Let me take you home. I think you're ill and don't realize it."

"It's true, it's true! Look, I was sitting under this tree here. . . ."

Steven looked around, puzzled, but Elizabeth continued, ignoring his confusion at her mention of the missing tree. "I was looking at the sun reflecting in my ring and—"

"That ring!" Steven interrupted. "Please let me see it."

She held out her hand, showing him the gold ring.

"That's my ring," he said. He reached for it hesitantly, and Elizabeth quickly withdrew her hand.

"I've been looking everywhere for it," he explained. "That's why I came to the graveyard today. I thought I might have dropped it the last time I visited my sister's grave. It was her ring and before she died she gave it to me. I carry it in my pocket all the time. Please may I have it back? That ring is all I have left of her. Please. Please give it back to me."

He reached out again. Elizabeth felt a wave of sympathy for this tall, gangly boy who cared so deeply for his lost sister.

"Sure," she said gently. "I'd be glad to give it back to you." She pulled at the ring, but it was stuck. She tried loosening it by turning it on her finger.

Suddenly, Steven was gone, swept away in the thick mist along with the new gravestones and the treeless hillside. Again, her head ached behind her eyes and her stomach churned. As soon as the sick feeling passed, she found herself back in the familiar 1980 cemetery.

The tall pine tree stood guard over the anonymous

grave once more and everything was the way it had been, the way it should be. And Steven was gone.

It's the ring, Elizabeth thought. *When I turn it around on my finger it makes the world change or makes me change so I think I'm seeing things from long ago. It's the ring that's doing it. It's the ring!*

Chapter 7

Elizabeth slept restlessly that night. She dreamed of large, misty figures that rose up over her bed, and once, she cried out, waking herself up. The next morning she dragged herself out of bed in answer to the alarm's persistent ringing, dressed, and made her way to the kitchen where her mother was preparing breakfast.

"Good morning, Elizabeth. What's the matter? You look miserable. Are you nervous about going to the new school?"

"No, Mom. School will be fine, I guess. I just didn't sleep well—had some bad dreams."

"Have your breakfast and you'll feel better. Aren't you wearing a dress for the first day of school? Those jeans look rather grubby."

Elizabeth drank her orange juice. "Mom, no one wears a dress to school anymore, except for Christmas concerts. Come on!"

"But you look so nice in a dress! Oh, well, I guess times have changed."

Times have changed! Elizabeth suddenly wasn't hungry anymore. Time had changed on her again yesterday, only this time it had been worse. She had met and spoken to someone from that other time. What was happening to her? Was she going crazy?

She looked at her hand. Yesterday she had removed the ring the moment she reached home and tucked it carefully away in her top drawer. Having convinced herself that it was the ring that was causing the time warp, or whatever it was, she was taking no chances on being suddenly transported one hundred years back in time while she slept. It was odd how bare her hand looked without it, though. Maybe she should put it back on. . . .

"Stop daydreaming, Elizabeth, and finish your breakfast. Get a move on! You have to do something with your hair before you go." Joan Connell smoothed her own gently curling hair. "You're so much like your father. Especially when you fall into one of your daydreams. Wake up and get moving."

Elizabeth walked slowly. In spite of what she had told her mother, she was nervous about going to a new school. The Wells-Barkerville school, just a short walk from the Jack O'Clubs, served all the school-aged children in the Wells area, from kindergarden to Grade Ten. It was a small school, only six rooms, and she had heard that many of the classes were multiples — two or more in one room. Until now she had never been part of a split class, and she had certainly never expected to be in one in her Grade Ten year.

She hoped there would be someone in her class who she would like. Last year, in the big high school she had attended in Vancouver, most of the girls her age were interested in talking about boys and make-up and buying record albums — no one read science fiction. She felt different from the other girls and had become a bit of a loner

48

over the last year, spending a great deal of time in the library and gradually withdrawing from the circle of friends she had known since elementary school.

Perhaps the kids here won't be so hung up on boys and clothes, she thought. *Styles in Wells seem to be about a year behind those in Vancouver, and nobody seems to care much about what they wear. Maybe I'll fit in better.* She arrived at the school and brushed past a cluster of small children who were giggling on the cement steps. Nervously, she pushed open the main doors and went in to find her classroom.

Grade Eight through Ten in the Wells-Barkerville school were in one room. There were only sixteen students in the three grades. Only six, including Elizabeth, were in the Grade Ten group — three girls and three boys. Elizabeth felt very much a stranger. Mrs. Carter, the teacher, made the introductions. Janice, a fat, pimply girl, hung her head and blushed. A tall blonde named Candy smiled and said that she was sure Elizabeth would find Wells terribly boring after living in the big city. The boys shuffled their feet awkwardly and muttered greetings before turning their backs to continue their own conversation.

Great, thought Elizabeth. *They look like a fascinating bunch. It should be a good year for friends.* She knew she shouldn't be so sarcastic. She had only just met them, after all. Maybe they would turn out to be interesting people once she got to know them better. She was here in Wells for the year, so she'd just have to put up with the school, like it or not.

Mrs. Carter dismissed the class at ten, the usual procedure for the first day of school. Elizabeth watched other students leave the room. Little knots of friends formed and hurried off. Janice mumbled something that could have been "good-bye" before rushing out the door, but the others were too busy talking to each other to say a word to Elizabeth.

Mrs. Carter gathered up her papers. "I hope you enjoy our little school, Elizabeth," she said. "It's a good class. I'm sure that you'll find some friends among the other students. Good-bye. See you tomorrow." Then she left the room.

The classroom was empty, except for Elizabeth, still at her desk. The laughter in the hall make her feel even more lonely. She fought back tears. *What's the matter with you, Margaret Elizabeth!* she thought. *You've been in the school for only an hour. What do you expect! Instant friends!* Most of the kids in her class had probably been together since kindergarten, and were in no hurry to introduce a newcomer to their little groups.

She picked up the school supply list, wondering if the Wells General Store with the sign that boasted that they sold Just Everything, would really have all the supplies she needed. Then she left the empty classroom.

After leaving the school, Elizabeth forgot all about making friends. All she could think about were her strange experiences in the graveyard. She had to find out if she could make the change in time happen again. The ring was the key. By turning it around on her finger she could travel to and from Steven Baker's time. She had been turning the ring yesterday when Steven and the old graveyard disappeared.

Today was her last chance to visit the graveyard until the weekend. School would begin in earnest tomorrow. She didn't think that she could go through three days of wondering about the ring, but not knowing for sure. She had to go back to the Barkerville cemetery and turn the ring around to see if the change would happen — and if Steven would be there. *If I do see him,* she thought, *I'll give him back the ring and then I'll be finished with the whole business. No more time changes, no more bad dreams, no more wondering if I'm going crazy.*

After lunch, when her mother had gone to work, Elizabeth took the ring from her drawer. She placed it carefully on her finger, making sure not to turn it, and set out on her bicycle for the Barkerville graveyard.

The heat wave that had made August so unbearable held through to the second day of September. It didn't seem to bother the chickadees that hopped and fluttered noisily among the headstones at the Barkerville graveyard, but Elizabeth was grateful for the shade the big pine tree provided at her favourite spot.

She sat cross-legged with her backpack pillowing her spine against the trunk of the tree and stared into the ring's jewel. "Okay," she told herself. "Let's do it. If I turn the ring and nothing happens, then I can write off the whole experience as a bad dream. If something does happen...." Unable to finish that thought, she braced herself against the tree, took another deep breath and slowly turned the small gold ring on her finger.

Nausea gripped her. Her stomach again threatened to rise into her throat. She clenched her eyes shut and groaned. *It is the ring,* she said to herself as the sick feeling subsided and she could once more open her eyes.

The familiar mist swirled around her, and as it disappeared, revealed once again the treeless hillside and new graves of the Barkerville cemetery.

It's not a dream! It does happen, and I can make it happen when I want to. I'm in a real-life science fiction story.

"Please don't be frightened this time."

Again the voice came from behind her, and again she jumped up and whirled around.

"Don't do that! You scared me half to death!"

Steven stood before her, an apologetic smile on his face. "I'm really sorry, Elizabeth, but you seemed to come out of nowhere. One minute I was sitting here reading, and the next minute I looked up and there you were. I don't know how I missed seeing you come into the graveyard. I

51

was watching for you, hoping I'd see you again today." He smiled, and this time she was able to smile back at him.

"I wondered if I'd see you, too, Steven. You must have thought I was crazy yesterday."

"Well," Steven rubbed the right side of his nose. "I think you had too much sun. But when you ran off so suddenly, I was worried about you. I spent an hour looking for you and finally gave up. Where did you hide, anyway? And why did you hide?"

"I didn't hide, Steven. I went... I went home."

"But you don't live in Barkerville," said Steven. "I asked everyone yesterday and no family named Connell has come to town recently. Does your father have a claim up Richfield way? Or further down on Williams Creek?"

Elizabeth was a little hurt that he hadn't believed she was from the future. But, of course he couldn't have believed her. No one in his right mind would accept the fact that he had just spent half an hour talking to a visitor from the future. She could hardly believe it herself.

"I tried to explain yesterday, Steven, but I guess I wasn't very clear. Sit down, and I'll try again. I know it's hard to believe, but I really am from 1980. That's why you couldn't find me yesterday. I just wasn't here. I went back to my own time."

Steven sat down beside her, a mixture of puzzlement and anger on his face. "I told you I don't care for practical jokes, Miss Elizabeth," he said. "I don't think it's mannerly of you to tease me like this."

"But Steven, I'm serious. Listen. It has something to do with the ring, with your ring. When I turn it around on my finger I go back to your time, and when I turn it around again I'm home in my time, 1980. It's sort of — well, I guess you could call it magic."

"I'm not a believer in magic, not that kind anyway. I think you're having a joke at my expense, and I don't care for it. If you'll kindly return my ring, I'll be leaving now. Your teasing seems to me to be uncalled for — and cruel."

He stood up and held out his hand for the ring. Elizabeth found herself blushing, suddenly aware that she did not want this boy, no matter where he was from, to think of her as cruel.

"I'm not teasing. Please believe me, Steven."

Then she had a frightening thought. If she gave the ring back to Steven, she might never be able to return to her own time. She'd be stuck in 1870!

"Please, please let me keep the ring," she said. "I don't think I can get home without it. Really I don't."

Steven looked down at her. "It was my sister's ring. She's buried here, in the other corner of the graveyard. She got mountain fever in the spring, the first year we were here, a year and a half ago. She gave me the ring when she was sick and I've carried it ever since. Amy was only ten, but she knew, when the fever got very bad, that she was going to die. Please, Miss Elizabeth, give me back my ring. It means a great deal to me."

"But I can't, Steven, I can't give it to you or I'll be stuck here for the rest of my life. It's my only way of getting back to my own time. Please let me keep it!"

"There you go again with your talk of other times. It isn't proper for a young lady to have such wild notions. Miss Elizabeth, there's a hospital at Marysville. Please come with me and see the doctor. I'll get my father's wagon and take you over, or we can walk. It's just down the road."

"No, Steven. I'm all right. I'm not sick."

"Well, if you aren't just trying to make a mockery of me with your talk of *time*, you must have some sort of brain fever. I don't know what to think of you...."

His voice trailed off and he looked very bewildered.

An idea flashed in Elizabeth's mind. She stood up and said, "Listen, Steven. If I can prove to you that I'm from 1980, then will you let me keep the ring? If I can really prove it to you?"

Steven laughed, a husky laugh that echoed through the

graveyard. "And how does one go about proving such an outlandish notion? What are you going to do? Take me to 1980 or wherever you say you're from and show me miracles? Certainly! If you can prove to me that you are from some future time, then you can keep the ring with my blessing — and *I'll* go to Marysville and have my brain fever treated."

Elizabeth thought desperately. How could she make him believe her? There must be some way, something that she could use as proof. She looked around her. *The headstones*, she thought. *If I can remember the name of someone who died in 1870 and I tell him that person is going to die, then when it happens, he'll have to believe me.*

She quickly tried to recall the epitaphs she had memorized on her first few trips to the graveyard: *Peter Gibson, the first man to be buried here? No. Steven already knew about him. What about the baby, the seven month old son of John and Emily Bowron? No, he didn't die until 1889.*

She thought harder. *Sacred to the memory of Donald Easter. 21 of September, 1864. Too long ago.*

What about William Giles? She remembered his epitaph clearly: Native of Missouri, U.S. But he died in 1868, or was it 1869? Well, what about Marie Hageman? Native of Germany, Rest in Peace. What was that date? 1888? Too far ahead.

Think, Elizabeth, think! she told herself. *You must have memorized fifty of those headstones. Surely there was someone who died in September of 1870.* She sat down again and pulled a strand of hair across her face, nibbling on it as she thought. Steven remained standing and staring at her, amused. *Think, Margaret Elizabeth, think!* she told herself again.

Then she had it! Janet Allen! The Judge had told her about 'Scotch Jenny' as she was known, and Elizabeth had searched out her grave and memorized the writing on the headstone. *Native of Fifeshire, Scotland. Who departed this life September 4, 1870, aged 42.* She could see the grave and the writing on the headstone clearly, even though in this graveyard it would not exist for a few days.

Excitedly, she turned towards Steven. "I think I *can* prove it to you, Steven. But it will be two days before you see the proof."

"Go ahead then. I'm listening." He settled himself down on the grass beside her, his long legs stretched out in front of him and his green eyes serious. "I'm listening," he repeated.

"Do you know a lady named Janet Allen who owns a saloon somewhere on Lightning Creek?"

"Of course," Steven replied. "Everyone knows 'Scotch Jenny'. She's a fine woman, always right there to help when a family is sick or in trouble."

"Oh." Elizabeth suddenly felt differently about telling Steven her proof. The name on the tombstone had become a real person, someone Steven knew and whose death would upset him. But she had to tell him. It was the only way to make him believe that she was from another time.

Taking a deep breath, she went on. "I'm sorry, Steven, but she's going to die on September 4, 1870. That's only two days from now, in your time. Her buggy is going to go over the bank into the creek and she's going to fall out and break her neck."

Steven's eyes widened in surprise and disbelief. "That's a horrible thing to say! It's like wishing death on a person to speak of such things. How can you talk like that?"

"I'm sorry," she repeated, "But it's true. I've seen her grave. She'll be buried right over there. I also know that she was so loved and respected that the flags in Barkerville were hung at half mast when she died."

"I don't believe you!" Steven looked angrily at her, one hand rubbing the side of his nose.

"I know it's hard to believe. But look. Today is September 2. Sunday will be the seventh. I realize you don't believe me now, but by then you will. Can you meet me here on Sunday, about the same time, about two? Let me

55

keep the ring until then and if you don't believe me by Sunday I'll give it back to you. Please, Steve?"

"Steve? My family calls me Steven."

"Well, Steven, if you prefer. I don't know why I said Steve."

"No. I like you calling me Steve." He shook his head, as if to shake away an upsetting thought.

"Very well, then. I don't believe you, and I pray to God that you aren't correct about Mrs. Allen, but I will meet you here on Sunday and you may keep the ring until then. Maybe by then I'll understand what's wrong with you, or maybe you will have come to your senses and stopped believing in this 'different times' nonsense."

"Thanks, Steve, thanks. I'll see you on Sunday, then. And don't worry. I'll take good care of the ring."

Smiling at him, she stood and deliberately turned the tiny ring on her finger. "Goodbye, Steve."

Then, after the nausea passed, she was home again. Back in her own time, back in the cemetery as it looked, or as it would look, in 1980.

Chapter 8

The rest of the week dragged by slowly. Elizabeth sat at her desk and obediently struggled with math problems, grammar exercises and Canadian geography, but her mind was somewhere else. She ate lunch with Janice one day. The big girl's painful shyness made her uncomfortable to talk to, and Elizabeth found that they spent most of the hour in silence.

She helped her mother in the restaurant one night, did more than her share of housework in the trailer, and even kept her room tidy most of the week. However, in spite of her attempts to stay busy and keep her mind off Steve and the graveyard, she found that she could think of little else. Would it really happen, she wondered? Would Barkerville's beloved Scotch Jenny fall from her carriage and break her neck on September 4, 1870?

Or maybe, as some science fiction authors suggested, Steve was from a *different* time stream. Maybe he was from a Barkerville that existed side by side with one in the history books, a Barkerville where Janet Allen would not die.

Somehow Elizabeth managed to get through the week. On Friday evening she baby-sat Fay, the MacDonald's baby, while the owner of the Jack O' Clubs and his wife went into Quesnel to do some shopping. Saturday, she again threw herself into the housework and surprised her mother by volunteering, for the second time that week, to help out in the restaurant.

"School has certainly been good for you, Elizabeth," her mother commented. "I don't know when you've been so nice to have around. You're awfully quiet, though. Is anything the matter, dear?"

Elizabeth shrugged off her mother's question with a smile. There was no way she could tell anyone, least of all her practical, realistic mother, what was wrong. She imagined the conversation:

"Well, Mom, I'm kind of worried because I seem to be able to go back in time. There's this boy I've met, from 1870, and I promised to give him back his ring, the one I found by the old grave. But if I do give it to him, I might be stuck in his time! So if I don't show up in time for dinner on Sunday, make sure you go back to *old* Barkerville to look for me, because that's where I'll be."

Her mother's reaction to that conversation would be to bundle Elizabeth off to see a psychiatrist! Her mother didn't believe in anything occult, but she had great faith in the miracles of modern medicine. If your body was ill, a regular doctor could fix it. If your mind was ill (if, for example, you were talking to people from the past), then a psychiatrist was the answer — and right away!

Sorry, Mom, she thought. *There is no way I can share this experience with you. You would think I was crazy for sure. And — maybe I am crazy! I may be absolutely nuts and don't realize it. What if Steve is a figment of my imagination and I haven't seen him or talked to him at all? What if I've just been sitting in the graveyard talking to myself?*

She couldn't let herself think this way. *Stop it,* she told herself firmly. *You'll just have to wait until Sunday and see what happens.*

Although it seemed to take forever, Sunday did at last come. Shortly after one o'clock she set out, somewhat nervously, for Barkerville.

The sun, after a month of almost continuous shining, refused to put in an appearance this afternoon. Grey clouds hugged the low hills around Wells, and threatened rain. Elizabeth hadn't told her mother where she was going, but had left a note on the table saying she had gone to Barkerville. *Just in case,* she told herself. *Just in case I don't come back from 1870.*

She could see her mother frantically searching the graveyard that evening, a flashlight in her hand, looking for her missing daughter. In Elizabeth's imagination, her mother's flashlight would suddenly light up a gravestone no one had noticed before. "Margaret Elizabeth Connell," the old inscription would read. "From parts unknown. Died of grief. Spent her short time in Barkerville crying in the cemetery. May she rest in Peace."

The vividness of her thoughts surprised her. *I mustn't get off on that track,* she told herself firmly. *Of course I won't get trapped in Steve's time. I won't give him the ring. I'll go back on my promise and use it to take me home again.* She snorted, disgusted with herself. *Suppose nothing happens today; suppose the graveyard doesn't change, and Steve doesn't appear.* She was worrying over nothing. *Wait,* she told herself. *Just wait and see what happens.*

There were only a few cars in the parking lot today. The threatening weather and the fact that the holidays were over had drastically reduced the number of visitors to Barkerville, even though it was Sunday, usually a busy day.

She made her way slowly up the trail to the graveyard, half-way inclined to turn around, go back to Wells and forget the whole thing. For some reason, however, she badly wanted Steve to believe her, to realize that she wasn't a cruel practical joker or a crazy person. So she kept on walking, towards the graveyard and whatever she would find when she turned the ring on her finger.

It was the same, only this time the sense of being sick to her stomach didn't seem as powerful and didn't last as long. The mist cleared, and again she looked at the Barkerville cemetery as it had been over a century ago. "It *is* real," she said aloud. "I'm not imagining it. It's *real!*"

She looked around for Steve, hoping he would be there. Then she saw him coming slowly towards her, a lanky figure dressed today in a respectable dark suit, but still wearing his work boots. His face was solemn. He didn't say anything but stood silently for a few minutes, just looking at her.

"You were right," he said at last, in a low voice. "It happened just as you said it would — the fall from the buggy, the broken neck, the flags at half mast. Scotch Jenny is dead!"

Elizabeth felt a wave of sympathy for this tall, awkward boy. His face looked tense and his eyes were red-rimmed, as if he'd had no sleep the night before. "I'm sorry, Steve. I'm sorry," she said softly.

"We buried her yesterday." He gestured, and through the grave markers she could see fresh earth piled up where there had been no grave on her last visit. "My mother was terribly upset. When my sister took ill, Mrs. Allen came and. . . . "

"I know. She was a good person. I'm sorry you're upset, Steve."

"I saw her in town on Wednesday. She was in the store, and I served her. It was yard goods she wanted, to make herself a new dress. She bought satin — blue, the most expensive we had. I kept looking at her and wondering if what you had told me was true. *You're going to die tomorrow*, I kept saying to myself.

"Maybe I brought it on her, the accident, by thinking that. Maybe it's my fault that she died. Maybe I could have warned her somehow...."

Elizabeth reached out a hand towards him. "It's not your fault, Steve, really it's not. She was going to die whether you knew about it or not. You couldn't have warned her, even if you had tried. Please don't feel badly about it. You're not responsible for her death. You just knew ahead of time that it was going to happen."

He looked at her strangely. "How did you know?" he whispered. "How did you know that she was going to die? Are you a witch? Tell me the truth! I have to know!"

"Of course I'm not a witch. I...."

"But you disappeared last Tuesday. I was watching you and suddenly you weren't there anymore. What *are* you?"

"I know it's hard to believe, but I *am* from another time, from the future, Steve. In my time, I heard the story of Mrs. Allen and how she died. I've seen her gravestone, that's how I knew when she would die."

"I can't believe you, I can't!" Steve rubbed his hand nervously across the right side of his nose. "You told me it would happen and it did, but I still can't believe that you are what you say you are."

She smiled. "I know. I felt the same way myself. When it first happened I thought I was going nuts."

"Nuts? I don't know that word, at least not the way you used it."

"You know. Crazy. Insane. Out of my mind — brain fever, maybe?"

"Yes. I understand." He was solemn. "I've wondered about myself, too. I thought that maybe I was having hallucinations or that I was sick. I even took a tonic, but it didn't help." He shook his head. "If I don't believe that you're a witch and have cast some sort of a spell on me...." He stopped and looked carefully at her for a moment. "You don't *look* much like a witch to me and I don't really believe in witches — then I have to believe that you're from another time. Some sort of a ghost of the future."

"Yes. Just think of me as 'The Ghost of Christmas Yet to Come'." Elizabeth laughed. "But I don't think I'm as frightening as he was."

"You know the works of Charles Dickens?" Steve seemed surprised.

"Oh, yes. I've read *A Christmas Carol* several times. We studied it in school in Grade 7. I've read *Oliver Twist* too, and I've seen the movie they made from it."

"Movie?" he asked. "What do you mean?"

Elizabeth started to laugh, then stopped herself. Of course Steve wouldn't know what a movie was — he had never seen one. He would know about cameras, but the first moving picture was a long way in his future yet. She opened her mouth to explain, then hesitated. Could she explain how a movie camera worked, how movies were made? Could she explain about Hollywood and movie stars and all of the things that made movies such a big part of her world?

For the first time Elizabeth became aware of the great difference between the two of them. The past hundred years had seen some of the most technical advances the world had ever known — cars, jets, space travel, television, radar and on and on. How could Steve, with his 1870 viewpoint, be expected to understand, or to believe, all that would happen in the next century?

"It's a kind of photograph, but it moves and tells a story...," she began, but Steve had lost interest for the moment.

"Do you know that Mr. Dickens is dead?" he asked. "He died in June, but we just heard news of it last month. It was written up in the Cariboo *Sentinel*."

"Yes. I mean no. I mean, yes, I knew he was dead, but I didn't know when he died." Again, the strangeness of the situation struck her. How could she carry on a conversation with this boy? What could they talk about? How much of the future should she tell him; how much did he want to know?

Steve was looking at her strangely. "I forgot. Of course

you know that Mr. Dickens is dead. He died a long time ago by your reckoning, didn't he?"

She nodded, but didn't answer.

"Seems to me," he continued, "that the two of us have a problem with our communications. You know things that I don't know, that I don't want to know, and. . . . "

He seemed to be convinced that Elizabeth was from a different time. This helped her feel more at ease with the situation.

"Listen." Steve's green eyes seemed to grow darker as he spoke. "I know it's strange, but I do believe you when you say that you're from the future. What you told me would happen to Mrs. Allen *did* happen, just the way you said it would. But I felt uncomfortable, knowing she was going to die and waiting for it. Then I felt so badly when she died, almost as if I should have stopped it somehow."

"I don't believe you could have stopped it, Steve. It had already happened. It was already the past."

"I don't know. But I do know that I don't want you to tell me what's going to happen in my future. Believing in you is hard enough for me! I don't want to have to go around knowing what will happen tomorrow or next year or a hundred years from now. I don't want the responsibility of knowing, the loneliness of not being able to tell anyone else. Because who would believe me?

"I don't want to know about your world, about the future! I don't think I can change anything and I don't want the knowledge. Please, don't speak to me of things that are outside of my own time!"

He reached out a slender, freckled hand and touched her gently on the cheek. "Please?" he repeated in a whisper. "Please don't tell me these things?"

Reaching up, she covered his hand with her own. "Of course I won't tell you what you don't want to know, Steve," she answered softly. "I was just worrying about it myself — how much to tell you and how much you'd want to know. It's much better this way, much better."

For a moment they stood that way, Steve's hand against

her cheek and her own hand nestled against his. Then, to her horror, Elizabeth felt herself blushing. She dropped her hand and turned away, trying to hide the flush of crimson that she knew was spreading over her face and neck. Steve stepped backwards and cleared his throat hesitantly.

"Uh... well... thank you, Elizabeth."

"You can call me Bess, if you like." Elizabeth could hardly believe her own ears. She, who had gone through fifteen years of insisting that people call her Elizabeth, was actually asking this boy, this near stranger, to call her by a nickname.

"Bess. That's pretty. Is that what your family calls you?" Steve seemed to have recovered his composure and sounded confident again.

"No. But I have a friend who does. It seems... it seems to be a name that goes with Barkerville, somehow. Sort of old fashioned and I thought that you...." Her voice trailed off. She cursed herself. No matter what she said, it seemed to come out wrong.

"Bess. I like the name." Then, much to her surprise, Steve began to laugh. His laughter grew and grew until it echoed through the bare graveyard and bounced off the empty hills. He sat down on the grass, too weak to stay on his feet. Pounding his fists on the earth, his body shaking, the laughter poured out of him.

"Oh... I... I'm sorry," he managed to gasp, unable to control his voice.

"What's wrong? What's so funny?" Elizabeth felt hurt. Here she had just made a fool of herself by asking him to use her nickname, and Steve's response was to sit down on the grass and howl with laughter. "I don't see anything funny about my name!"

"No, believe me, it's not that!" Steve sat up and wiped his eyes. Tears were running down his face and he hiccupped, trying to restrain his laughter so that he could speak. "Oh, no, it isn't your name at all. It's a fine name. I was thinking how I'd tell my family about you at dinner tonight. 'I had an unusual day,' I'd say. 'I met this girl, Bess, in the graveyard and we had an interesting conversation.'

"Then my mother would say, 'A young lady, Steven? Where is she from?' and I would say, 'Oh, from about a hundred years in the future.'" He giggled again. "I'm sorry for laughing. It wasn't mannerly. But I could just imagine my mother's face if I told her about you. I couldn't help myself — I had to laugh!"

In spite of herself, Elizabeth giggled, too. "I know what you mean," she said. "I can just see *my* mother, too. 'Why don't you bring this Steve over to the trailer to meet me, Elizabeth?'" Then she began to laugh as well. The two of them sat on the grass and laughed until they could barely move.

Overhead, the sun broke through the threatening clouds and tossed light down to the earth. The chickadees seemed louder, as if they, too, shared the joke, and a robin, startled by the noise, hopped indignantly away.

The graveyard, usually the most silent and sombre of places, echoed with the laughter of two young people and the cheerful chorus around them.

Chapter 9

September 21, 1980
Sunday evening.

Dear Diary,

I never thought that I would be writing a diary. I always thought that it was a pointless thing to do and that I would be better off spending my time writing stories or letters or something useful. However, here I am, beginning a diary — well, an exercise book anyway. I won't give my diary a ridiculous name, like Anne Frank did, but I do feel the need to write down what I am feeling, to tell someone all about it.

The problem is that I have no one to talk to about Steve, no one on earth that I can tell about him. I suppose I could tell the Judge. He, more than anyone else, would be likely to understand. But I'm afraid that even the Judge won't believe me, won't understand. I mean, would anyone believe that I am meeting a boy from 1870? It sounds insane!

I've seen Steve twice more since that Sunday when he finally believed that I am from the future. We meet on Sundays when he doesn't have to work in his father's store, and we spend all afternoon in the graveyard. In spite of me not being able to mention the wonders of the twentieth century, we seem to find lots to talk about — and to laugh about. Today I forgot all about the time, so I was late getting home and Mom was really angry with me. She didn't have to work this Sunday evening and we were going to do some sewing together. I didn't get home until almost seven and it was beginning to get dark. She was furious.

It seems strange that Steve and I can find so much to talk about, but we do. People and families don't seem to have changed much in a hundred years, even if science and technology have. Steve's told me a lot about his little sister, Amy. She died the first spring they were in Barkerville, and he still misses her terribly. I wonder if today's doctors and modern medicines could have saved her? I've never had anyone close to me die. It must be a hard thing to go through.

He's also told me about coming to Barkerville just after the Great Fire in 1868. The store that they were going to buy had burned down and they had to rebuild it. The whole town seems to have been rebuilt very quickly after the fire. It's no wonder there weren't any trees around the town — they were all used for building.

I've been able to talk to Steve about my Dad. I still miss Dad a lot, even after nearly three months. I am able to tell Steve things that I can't tell anyone else. He doesn't laugh at me or tell me to snap out of it, the way Mom does. I haven't had a friend like Steve ever in my life. Not that the Judge isn't a great person, but he's so much older and besides he's spending a lot of time with Mom lately — if you can believe it! But Steve is different, and very special. He makes the boys at school seem like overgrown children with their dumb music and sports. When he gets serious about something his eyes seem to turn a darker green and he rubs the side of his nose where he broke it when he was six.

Oh, oh! I'm sounding like Candy from school who is always talking about boys and how cute they are and how crazy she is about this one or that one.

Time to go to bed, I guess. It's been good to write this down. I wish I could see Steve more often than on Sundays, even if it is every Sunday. I wish I could tell someone about him. I wish — oh, well. Good night.

October 5, 1980
Sunday night.

Dear Diary,

I haven't done much writing in you, have I? Well, I didn't promise to write every day, just when I needed someone to talk to. And mostly when I needed someone to talk to about Steve. I haven't written about our last few meetings, but today something strange happened and I need to talk about it.

It was cold today when I went up to the graveyard, and I was wearing a funny hat that Mom crocheted for me last year and jeans and my hiking boots. Steve laughed at me and said that I didn't look like a young lady at all but rather like one of the miners who comes into the store. Then he got a funny look in his eye and said, "Hey! You're dressed just right. Why don't we go down into town and you can see what Barkerville is like in my time?"

I laughed and said it wouldn't work, but then I started wondering what Barkerville in 1870 would look like. "Why not," I said. I made sure my hair was tucked up under my hat and we went out of the graveyard. Steve kept his eyes on me as we walked down the trail. The further we went, the more his expression changed to one of astonishment. Finally he stopped and said in a tight voice, "Bess, I don't think we should go any further." I laughed and called him a chicken, but he just stared at me strangely and said, "Look at your hand, Bess. Look at your hand!"

I looked, and I nearly died. I almost wasn't there! I mean I could see my hand, but I could see right through it as well. I could see the pebbles on the path right through my skin! I thought I was going to be sick for a moment, and I put my hands to my face. It was still there. I could feel it. Only the ring on my finger remained totally visible. The rest of me — clothes, boots, everything — had sort of melted into a mist of some kind. Steve said that he could see right through me!

69

I got frightened and turned around to go back. I was afraid that I would disappear completely. Then Steve tried to grab my hand, but he couldn't hold on to it! My hand just wasn't there, at least not for him. I could feel it fine though.

For a few seconds, he stood there with a stupid look on his face and kept trying to grab my hand. His hand swept right through mine as if it were smoke. I could feel his hand sort of brush mine, but he couldn't feel my hand at all.

We both ran back to the graveyard, scared, and I think I was almost crying. The closer we got to our special spot the more real I looked. By the time we got there I was totally visible and solid again.

Then — well, he took my hand and he could feel it because he said it was smooth and soft. He held it and pulled it to his face and, very gently, he turned it over and kissed the palm. "I was afraid I'd lost you." That was all he said. We stood there and sort of looked at each other for a while, and I felt myself beginning to blush. Then he dropped my hand and said, "You'd better go home now."

I went. Now I'm here in bed, writing all this down, and trying to understand what happened.

Why do I turn into a ghost away from the graveyard? Is it because it was there that I found the ring? The ring seems to exist in both of our times. I mean, Steve lost it in 1870 and I found it in 1980 but it couldn't have been lying there for all those years or someone else would have found it, I'm sure. Does the ring have some sort of power over the change in time that only works in that one spot? I don't understand at all. I don't think I'll try to go down the hill to Barkerville again, though. I wonder if I'd disappear into thin air? We'll both stay right there, at our special spot in the graveyard, and forget about the rest of the world, his time and my time.

He kissed my hand!

October 26, 1980
Sunday night.

Dear Diary,
   It got really cold today in the graveyard. It's been getting colder every Sunday for the last three weeks, and today it was bitter! I wonder if it is 1980 weather or 1870 weather at the cemetery. Does the weather change too, when I turn the ring? It always seems the same in Steve's time as it is in my time. I guess I'll never know for sure.
   Mom was really mad at me for going to Barkerville today. She says that she can't understand what the fascination is with a deserted old graveyard in almost the middle of winter and why don't I stay home Sundays and have some friends over.
   That's fine for her to say. She and the Judge went into Quesnel for dinner and a show yesterday, and she's joined an artists' group and goes to meetings once a week with her easel and paints. She isn't stuck in this awful town with only five other people her own age.
   Anyway, the cold worked out well today because Steve and I sat close together. He put his arms around me and held me next to him while we talked. It was such a warm, comfortable feeling to be sitting there with him, snug in spite of the cold.
   We talked. We were both wondering how long we can go on meeting here. Winter is on its way, and there will be a lot of snow and temperatures down to minus forty! Since the weather seems to be the same in both our times, we decided that we'd be sensible about it and not even try to meet if it's too cold. I hope it never gets too cold!
   Anyway, we talked and we laughed. Then, just before I left he put his hand under my chin and sort of tilted back my head and kissed me. I blushed; I know I did because he laughed and said he didn't mind my blushing, that it was "maidenly".
   Oh, dear Diary, I really am in trouble. I think I'm falling in love! But how can I fall in love with someone who doesn't exist. I mean, of course he exists. He kissed me, didn't he? But he doesn't exist here and now and he can

never be here, in Wells, with me. He can never meet my Mom or take me to a dance or a movie. He's dead, in my time. Even if he lived to be a hundred years old he would have died almost thirty years ago! I can't fall in love with someone who isn't alive, can I? Oh, I don't know what I mean. I'm happy and sad all at once and at the same time I know the whole thing is impossible and should never be happening. What am I going to do? What am I going to do? Oh, Steve.

November 23, 1980
Sunday night.

Dear Diary,

Today was the first time for three weeks that Steve and I have been able to meet. I missed him, very much; almost as much as I miss Dad. It got very cold late in October and I couldn't go to Barkerville. Then it began to snow. It snowed and it snowed and it snowed! We never had snow like this in Vancouver. It just kept on coming down, day after day. All the roads in town have been cleared but every empty lot is piled up with snow well over my head. I wonder when it will finally all be gone? In the spring? May? June?

As soon as it started to snow, all the kids hauled out their cross-country skis and started skiing everywhere — even to school. I'd never been on any kind of skis before, but Janice lent me hers one day and helped me a bit. It's fun, and not nearly as hard as I thought it would be. You have to learn how to glide then give a little push. Once you get the rhythm it's quite easy. The hardest part is learning how to handle those great long skis so you aren't tripping over your toes all the time.

I guess Mom is trying to make up for being so bad tempered lately, because she went into Quesnel and bought me my own set of skis and boots. Even a warm jacket with matching pants. (You wear short pants, sort of like knickers, for cross-country skiing, with long, thick wool socks.) The outfit is blue, and the skis are the kind that never have to be waxed before you use them, so all I have to do is put them on and off I go.

I spent a lot of time learning to ski, and today it warmed up to just below freezing and I wondered if I could make it to Barkerville on skis. I'd done the eight kilometers often enough on my bike, and I thought I could manage it on my skis. I figured that it would be warmer in Steve's time, too, and he would go to the graveyard hoping that I could get there. I wanted to see him so much!

So, after Mom had gone to work, I got dressed in my ski outfit, filled a canteen with juice and packed an extra pair of mitts and a small thermal blanket in my backpack, and started out.

I thought that I had become a pretty good skier, but those eight kilometers were hard to manage. There was a skidoo trail beside the road all the way into Barkerville, but it was slick and icy in some spots and I took some bad falls. But, I kept on going and finally reached the grave-yard trail. I left my skis at the foot of the trail. There was no way I was ready to try that steep trail, either up or down, with skis on!

The climb up was hard, too. Someone had plowed some sort of trail, but there had been a new snowfall and it wasn't much of a path. I was exhausted and covered with snow by the time I reached the cemetery.

I waded through the deep snow between the graves, turning myself into a sort of human snow plow. Finally, I reached the big pine tree and my special grave. The grave-yard looked so different covered with snow. The tomb-stones seemed to be only half their regular height and wore tall white caps that made them look like they were wearing costumes. The wooden fences around the graves were half buried in snow and looked as if they had been iced with fluffy white icing. It was pretty, in a strange sort of way, but seemed lonelier than it did before the snow came.

Well, I turned the ring. I guess it was because I haven't made the change for a while, because I felt dreadfully sick this time. When everything settled down, I opened my eyes, and as the mist cleared I could see Steve! I ran to him as quickly as I could in the deep snow, and he picked me up and hugged me and said, "I was hoping you would come today, Bess. I've missed you so much!" Then he gave me a long kiss, still holding me up so my feet didn't touch the ground.

Oh, dear Diary, it was so good to see him again! I was sweaty and tired from the trip and my muscles were beginning to stiffen up, but I felt like singing!

We scooped away a hollow in the snow and I spread the insulating blanket. Steve made fun of my ski outfit, especially the boots with the long toes and the three holes that the skis latch into. We talked and laughed and tried to hold hands without taking off our mitts. Finally Steve pulled my ski mitt off and took my hand in his and covered both of them with the scarf he had been wearing around his neck. The sun was shining, making the snow throw off little sparkles, and chickadees were singing in a bush nearby. I felt happier than I'd ever felt in my life!

Then we suddenly heard a voice calling from the entrance to the graveyard! We both jumped, and turned around to listen. There had never been anyone else in the graveyard before when Steve and I met. Sound carries easily through the winter air and we could hear the words clearly. "Steven? Steven, are you there?"

Chapter 10

The voice startled both of them. Steve jumped to his feet, a look of panic on his face. "It's my mother," he said. "What are we going to do?"

This was something they hadn't planned on. No one except Steve had ever come to the 1870 graveyard while Elizabeth was there, and they were unprepared for dealing with a visitor. They looked at each other for a few seconds, wondering how to handle the situation. "I'll go," said Elizabeth and picked up the blanket and pulled off her other mitt so she could turn the ring.

"No. Please don't go yet. You've only just arrived, and it's been so long since I've seen you. Stay."

Elizabeth thought quickly. "I could come back when she's gone," she said.

"But how will you know when she's gone? In your time you can't see her. You might come back when she's still here and that would frighten both of you. Besides I'd like you to see my mother, even if you can't meet her."

He picked up her backpack. "Here. The snow is deep

enough so that if you crouch down behind a gravestone she won't notice you." As quickly as he could in the deep snow he led the way to Chartres Brew's grave. "Mother is coming to visit Amy's grave, I'm sure. It's over in the other corner. Just stay here and be still and she won't notice you. I'll get her to go home as quickly as I can."

Elizabeth scooped a small hollow in the snow behind the headstone and settled herself down. "Okay. I'll wait. But I feel like a criminal or something. Just call me 'Bess the Burglar'."

Steve smiled, then turned and made his way to the graveyard gate. "I'm over here, Mother," he called.

Cautiously, Elizabeth peered over the top of the headstone. Steve was walking towards a woman in a long dress which she lifted slightly in front of her with one hand, trying to keep it out of the snow. Her blonde hair was partly covered by a long shawl which her other hand grasped tightly at her chest. She did not wear a coat, and her hands were bare, as if she'd left home without dressing properly for the long walk.

"Steven?" Her voice was low, but carried clearly across the deserted graveyard. "Steven, I thought you would be here." Steve reached her and she took his arm, looking up at him. She was a short woman, and very slender.

Steve must get his height from his father's side of the family, Elizabeth thought. She watched as the two of them walked towards the far side of the graveyard.

"You have been to visit Amy's grave again, haven't you Steven?" Although her voice was gentle she seemed to be reproaching him. "You come here nearly every Sunday, my son. Can you not let go of the past and cease your mourning?"

They had made their way slowly to a small grave with a wooden cross at its head. As they stood beside it, Steve put his arm around his mother's shoulders. "I'm not grieving for Amy, Mother. I mean, I do miss her, very much, but I'm not keeping vigil over her grave."

"Then why are you spending so much time here, Steven? Why do you isolate yourself from your family, and on Sundays, too, the day when families can be together and draw strength and comfort from each other?"

Their backs were to Elizabeth as she risked another look over the top of the headstone. The short woman had her hand on Steve's arm and looked up at him. Even at this distance, Elizabeth could sense the woman pleading with her son.

"I'm sorry, Mother. I *do* spend the morning with you and Father and go to church with you."

"Steven, Steven," his mother sighed. "Something is wrong with you. It's not natural for a young man to spend so much time alone, and in a graveyard. I thought you had recovered from your obsession with this place, for you have stayed home with us for three Sundays. But today, when you left, I knew where you were going. You must forget her, son, and live your own life. Let her go. Let her go."

Elizabeth could see Steve's shoulders move as he started in surprise. She was startled, too. How could Steve's mother know about her? What had happened?

"How . . . how do you know, Mother?"

"I know many things, son. It comes from being a mother and having that closeness to my children that only a mother's love can bring."

"But I can't just let her go, Mother. She . . . she means a great deal to me. I only see her on Sundays and —"

"*See* her?" His mother's voice was harsh. "Do you have visitations? Do you believe that you can actually see the ghost of your dead sister?"

"Sister?" Steve's sigh of relief sounded loud in the graveyard. "Oh, no, Mother. You mistake me. I didn't mean that I can see Amy. She was a gentle child who would never assume the aspects of a spectre — even if such things were possible."

"Then whom *do* you see, Steven? Whom do you meet

here in this place of the dead?"

"Someone . . . no one! No one at all! Oh, Mother I can't explain it to you." His voice was low and tense. "I come here just to — to find peace and solitude. Here no one cares about staking claims or finding the mother lode. Here the noise and bustle of Barkerville seem so far away and unimportant."

"You have your room and your books. Can you not find solitude in your own home, near those who love you?"

"Yes, but —"

"I worry for you Steven. You have changed over the past few months. You have become quiet, and seem to be drawing away from your father and me. It's as if you were leading a life of your own; a life that is far removed from the world you actually live in. It's unnatural for someone of your age!"

"Mother, you mustn't worry! I'm very happy."

"Happy? Here, alone in a graveyard? Oh, Steven, come back to us. Forget about this place. Give up your visits here, your unhealthy search for solitude. And — mourn no more for Amy. She is content now. It's time for you to be content, too."

"Mother, I. . . . " Steve's arm tightened around her shoulders and he pulled her closer to him. "I care for you and Father very much, you know that. But I *must* keep on coming here. It is something that is very important to me and I can't give it up."

Steve's mother gently pushed herself away from him. "Steven, I was hoping that you would make the decision on your own. However, I see that you will not, so I must tell you. Your father has forbidden you to come to the graveyard again, unless you come with one of us. He believes, as I do, that you are still grieving for your sister and he is afraid that this grief will make you ill. Although you are seventeen and of a man's stature, you still have to obey your father."

"But Mother, I can't stop coming here! Please reason

with Father. Speak to him. Make him realize that my visits here are not harmful — "

"I am sorry, Steven, but I agree with your father. These continual visits to your sister's grave are unhealthy and unnatural. They must cease!"

She gathered her skirt with one hand and pulled her shawl closer about her. "Come with me now. It grows cold and darkness will soon begin to fall." Turning, she began to make her way carefully through the snow, back to the gate.

"I can't go now, Mother, I can't!" Steve looked desperately towards where Elizabeth was hiding. "Please. Give me just a few more minutes."

"Follow me down the trail, Steven. I expect you home shortly after I arrive there myself." Her voice faded as she left the graveyard and started down the path.

Elizabeth stood up and Steve came to her quickly, in leaps that carried him easily through the deep snow. "Bess, oh, Bess!" he cried and once more swept her up into his arms.

"What are we going to do, Steve?" she whispered against the rough wool of his jacket. "What are we going to do now?"

Elizabeth stared at the diary in front of her. She couldn't write anymore.

After Steve's mother had left the graveyard, they had talked anxiously for a short time. Now that Steve had been forbidden to go to the graveyard it meant that they couldn't meet at all — unless he lied to his parents and went against his father's wishes. Steve didn't want to do that. He had never lied to his parents before, and the thought of having to do it upset him. Yet, he wanted to be able to see Elizabeth as much as she wanted to see him.

Elizabeth sighed, then put the diary away, under her mattress. There was no point in worrying about it now, there was nothing she could do. She and Steve had agreed not to meet for a few weeks, until Sunday, December 14. Then, if the weather were warm enough, she would go to the graveyard — and Steve would, too. He promised that he would find a way to be there, in spite of his parents' orders.

She felt angry and depressed. She and Steve had enough problems with their relationship as it was, and now he was forbidden to go to the one place where they could meet. It wasn't as if they could see each other more often, go on dates, talk on the phone. It wasn't a normal friendship at all.

Friendship? She smiled, thinking that by now the two of them had more than that, much more. Before he left the graveyard, Steve had kissed her, holding her face gently in his hands. Then, just as she turned the ring to come back to her own time, she heard him say, "I love you, Bess. I love you!"

Chapter 11

The next day dragged by. Elizabeth could not concentrate on her school work, but kept worrying about Steve. What would he do now that he had been forbidden to go to the graveyard? What would she do if she couldn't see him again? Instead of paying attention to what was happening in class, she found herself daydreaming about the two of them, about the way their relationship was changing and growing. She was more fond of Steve than she had ever been of anyone.

Let's face it, she told herself. *You're in love with him. In love! Well, maybe.* Smiling, she thought of how she'd never paid much attention to her friends in Vancouver when they moaned about being in love. *I guess I never really knew what it was all about. I never realized how much a part of you someone else can become, and how you can miss someone so much.*

She looked down at the ring. It was the beginning of the whole problem. If she had never found it she wouldn't be in such a state now.

I wonder if it only works in the graveyard! she thought. Almost before she realized what she was doing she turned it around on her finger. The classroom swam before her eyes and her stomach wrenched. Her head ached viciously and the familiar mist welled up, obscurring the faces of her classmates. But nothing else happened! Through the mist she could still see the classroom, the teacher, and the familiar objects of her own time. She was still in 1980.

Frantically, she turned the ring again and the mist faded, her stomach settled, and the piercing headache eased.

"Elizabeth, are you all right?" Mrs. Carter, her teacher, was standing over her, a look of concern on her face. "You suddenly turned pale and began to slump forward in your seat. Are you feeling all right?"

"Yes." Elizabeth rubbed her hands across her eyes. "it was just a . . . a headache. I'm fine now."

"You don't look fine. You look ghastly." Mrs. Carter reached out and touched her forehead. "Why, you're ice cold! I think you must be ill, Elizabeth. Come on. Let's find someone to drive you home. You belong in bed."

Mr. Jackson, the principal, helped Elizabeth into his old station wagon. "It's going around, right now," he said. "A nasty flu. Have a few days in bed and you'll feel more like yourself."

He drove carefully through the icy streets and dropped her behind the Jack O' Clubs hotel, at the door of the trailer. "Are you sure you'll be all right?" he asked. "Would you like me to get your mother from the restaurant?"

"It's okay." She managed a weak smile. "Mom hasn't gone to work yet, so she'll be here. Thanks for the ride home."

"Sure. Take care now." With a wave and a friendly grin he pulled away, leaving her standing in front of the trailer.

"That was a stupid thing to do," Elizabeth told herself. She still felt weak and the remnants of the headache nagged behind her eyes. Nothing had happened when she turned the ring except that she felt terrible. She had never felt quite that sick before. Whatever the magic or power the ring had, it only worked in the graveyard. She decided never to try the time change anywhere else again.

Walking slowly up the stairs to the front door, she opened it and went in. "It's me, Mom, I'm not — "

Her mother was sitting at the kitchen table, a cup of coffee in front of her, and Elizabeth's diary in her hand!

"Elizabeth!" She looked up, startled. "What are you doing here? I thought you were at school. I was just ... " Her voice trailed off as she looked down at the exercise book in her hand.

"Mother! That's mine! What are you doing with my diary?" Elizabeth's voice rose in anger, her weakness and headache forgotten as the full impact of her mother's actions hit her. "How could you do such a thing? How could you be such a — a snoop?"

"Elizabeth, I'm sorry dear. I can explain. You see, I decided to do a laundry and I went to get your sheets. This was under your mattress and — "

"But it says PRIVATE right on the cover. You've no business reading it!"

"I know, but I've been so worried about you lately and I thought — "

"Being worried doesn't give you the right to read my diary!"

"I know, I know dear, but I had to do something, had to find out what was upsetting you."

"You've always said that members of a family have to respect each other's privacy, and now you turn around and do something like this." Elizabeth was near tears. She was furious with her mother, but more than that she was worried about how much her mother had read in the diary. If her mother had read all about the ring, the time changes and Steve, she'd be convinced that Elizabeth was having a nervous breakdown or going crazy.

"Please, Elizabeth, try to understand. I did what I

83

thought best. You've been so withdrawn lately, so unlike yourself. And you've been spending so much time in that graveyard at Barkerville. I've been very concerned.

Oh, no! Elizabeth thought. *She sounds just like Steve's mother! Why can't our parents leave us alone!*

Her mother went on, hesitantly. "Even yesterday, when it was so cold, you went up there and stayed for a couple of hours. I was just trying to find out what was bothering you."

"You could have asked me, you know, instead of sneaking around behind my back and reading my diary!"

"But Elizabeth, I *have* asked you, and you keep telling me that nothing's wrong."

"Nothing *is* wrong," snapped Elizabeth, "Except that I can't trust my own mother. Now, please may I have my diary back?"

"Here." Her mother handed it to her. "Please sit down, Elizabeth. We have to talk about . . . about what I've read."

"It's none of your business and I don't want to talk about it!" Clutching her diary to her chest, Elizabeth walked past her mother, towards her bedroom.

"Elizabeth." Joan Connell reached out a hand and held her shoulder, preventing further retreat. "We have to talk about these hallucinations of yours."

"They're not hallucinations and I don't want to talk." Elizabeth shook off her mother's hand and turned her back. "I don't want to talk to you ever again. Let me alone!"

Running to her room she slammed and locked the door and threw herself on the bed. *I'm being childish*, she thought, *very childish.* Then she began to cry.

The tears must have stopped, although Elizabeth couldn't remember when. She remembered her mother knocking on the door, calling, "Please, dear. Unlock the door. Please, Elizabeth."

She must have cried herself out and fallen asleep. Now her room was dark and through the small window she could see that the day was over. She sat up in bed; her eyes felt puffy and swollen. Although still angry at her mother, she was now more worried than anything else.

I'll get up and wash my face, she thought. *Then I'll go over to the restaurant and I'll make up some story to tell Mom. Maybe I can get her to believe that I'm writing a story, not a diary at all, and that it's supposed to be happening to a fictitious character. It's all I can do. I have to persuade her that I'm not crazy, that I'm not having hallucinations.*

While she was washing her face with cold water, trying to erase the signs of her long session of tears, she heard voices. Her mother had returned to the trailer and had brought someone with her. Elizabeth listened carefully, trying to identify the other voice. Then she heard it clearly. "Yes, Joan. I'll be glad to talk to her. Relax." It was the Judge.

Her mother must have told him everything — about the diary and Steve. Now she'd have to face him as well as her. She didn't want to see either of them, but the sooner she got it over with, the sooner things would, hopefully, return to normal. Taking a deep breath, she opened the bathroom door and went into the kitchen.

"Elizabeth!" Her mother rushed over and hugged her. "Are you feeling better, dear? I thought you'd never stop crying. Oh, Elizabeth. . . . " Her mother's voice was tearful as she held Elizabeth and brushed back a strand of hair that had fallen across her face.

"It's okay, Mom. Hello, Judge." She sat down at the table. "Could I have a cup of coffee, please? It might wake me up. I haven't slept in the afternoon like that since I had measles." She smiled weakly, and her mother smiled back.

"Sure. We'll all have a cup." Joan Connell busied herself making coffee while Elizabeth sat, trying not to meet the Judge's questioning eyes.

"Uh, Mom? That diary? It's not really *my* diary. It's just a story I'm making up and writing down, that's all. . . . "

"Oh, Elizabeth. You know that's not true. It is your diary, you said so yourself. You have to face the fact that you have a problem, dear. Don't try to run away from it."

"Bess?" The Judge's voice was gentle. "Why didn't you come and talk to me? I thought we were friends?"

"I couldn't, Judge. I knew that no one, not even you, would believe me. I just couldn't talk to you. I'm sorry."

"Can you tell me about it now, Bess. All of it? I only know what your mother has told me, what she read in your diary. Will *you* tell me?"

While her mother prepared and served the coffee, Elizabeth sat with her head bowed and slowly told the whole story: about the ring, about the way the 1870 graveyard looked, about Steve and about Steve again. The Judge and her mother listened, not interrupting her story, their faces serious. "That's what happened," Elizabeth concluded and, for the first time, raised her eyes to look at them.

Her mother wore a tight, closed look on her face, tension lines showing at the corners of her mouth. The Judge was solemn, his eyes narrowed in thought, one hand tugging gently at his beard. "You don't believe me, do you? You don't believe me." For the second time that day she fought back tears.

"Oh, Elizabeth," Joan Connell reached out for Elizabeth's hand, holding it firmly in her own. "Of course we believe that you *think* you've been seeing all these things. But you do know, don't you, that you're just imagining it? No one can go back in time, in spite of what those science fiction books of yours say. It just can't happen."

"I'm not imagining it, Mom. It's real! I *do* see Steve and time *does* change!"

"Bess, I wish you'd spoken to me earlier. Maybe I could have helped." The Judge looked at her, his eyes kind.

"You believe me, don't you, Judge? You said yourself that Barkerville has a powerful sense of history and that sometimes you feel as if the real Judge Begbie were taking over your body. You believe me, don't you?"

"I don't know, Bess. I know that the past in Barkerville is very close to the present, and that many people have strange feelings when they're in the town. However, I've never heard of anyone actually going back in time."

"But Judge, it does happen, really it does!"

"You've been very lonely since you came to Wells, Bess. Maybe your imagination has created Steve — someone to be your friend. Loneliness can do strange things to people."

"It's my fault!" Joan Connell broke in. "I never should have taken her away from Vancouver. It's all my fault that this has happened."

"Nonsense, Joan!" said the Judge. "It isn't your fault at all. We all know that Bess has a very vivid imagination. Barkerville has just stimulated that imagination, that's all."

"Oh, Judge! You *don't* believe me. And I thought that you, of all people, would understand." Elizabeth felt betrayed. She had been sure that she had a friend in the Judge, someone who would help her convince her mother. Now, he seemed almost to be taking her mother's side in believing that Steve didn't exist.

"Listen, both of you," said the Judge. "I have an idea that might help you to solve this problem. "I can't say that I believe you, Bess. That is, I believe *you*, but I'm not sure whether I believe that Steve exists in the real world, or just in your imagination. And Joan," he turned to Elizabeth's mother, "you know that Bess is a pretty level headed person, not someone likely to have hallucinations. I don't believe you either when you say that she's gone crazy."

Joan Connell's lips tightened. "Well, if you don't believe either one of us, what do *you* think is happening?"

"I don't know, Joan. But I have an idea that might work. I'll go to the graveyard with Bess. Let me see what happens when she turns her ring."

Joan Connell snorted. "You're sounding as if you

believe that something *will* happen."

"We won't find out until we try, will we?" The Judge smiled. "If something does happen then we'll know that Bess is right, and you and I, Joan, will have to adjust our thinking to accept time travel." He smiled again. "I'd love to go back to 1870."

"And what if nothing happens?" asked Elizabeth in a small voice.

"Then, Bess, you owe it to your mother to try her solution."

"Yes." Joan Connell took over the conversation. "I want to take you to see a doctor, Elizabeth. A psychiatrist. I've already phoned and made an appointment for you to see Dr. Fendell in Quesnel on Friday. I think you need help, my dear, very badly."

"A psychiatrist! But, Mom. . . . " Elizabeth began to protest, then thought better of it. After all, once the Judge had seen the time change himself her mother would know that she wasn't crazy. They could always cancel the appointment. "Okay," she said. "I agree. When will you come to the graveyard with me, Judge?"

"How about tomorrow, after school? We'll go right away so the light doesn't fade before we've seen... seen whatever there is to see." He sat back in his chair and gave a sigh of relief. "Now, let's all forget about it and go over and have dinner. Your mother has to get back to work; she took a few hours off because she was worried about you, especially when she heard that you were ill in school this morning."

"I'm better now. I told you why I was sick — I tried to turn the ring and it didn't work."

"We won't talk about it right now, Elizabeth," said her mother firmly. "I do have to get back to work. Comb your hair. Then you and the Judge come over and eat. There's clam chowder, your favourite. We won't speak of your... experiences... again tonight. We'll wait and see what happens tomorrow."

Chapter 12

The Judge drove Elizabeth to Barkerville the next afternoon, and together they fought through the snow that covered the steep trail to the graveyard. Elizabeth was very nervous and had worried most of the night over what would happen today. Steve wouldn't be in the graveyard. It was Tuesday, and they met only on Sundays. Besides, he had been forbidden to go to the cemetery and they had agreed to wait until December 14 before trying to meet again. But the new-looking graves would be there and the headstones of those who had died after 1870 would not be there. That should be enough proof to convince the Judge.

She talked rapidly to cover her nervousness. "I wish you could meet Steve, Judge, but he won't be expecting me today and he won't be there. You'd like him. He works in his father's store, but he'd really like to be a doctor. He's very smart. Sometimes he goes with Dr. Black on his rounds and he reads all sorts of medical books. I could tell him a lot of things about science and medicine that would help him in his studies, but I promised not to talk about things that would happen in the future. It makes him feel uneasy to know what is going to happen, like when he knew about Scotch Jenny before she died. When he's older he hopes to go away to study and then...."

Her voice trailed away. They reached the gate to the cemetery, and the Judge stood beside it, smiling at her. "Where is this special grave of yours, Bess? Show me where the magic of the ring works."

"Over there." Elizabeth pointed, and the two of them began to push their way through the deep snow, following the indefinite trail that she had made in earlier visits. The Judge brushed the snow from the wooden marker.

"I don't know this grave," he said. "The lettering has nearly worn away and what's left is covered with moss. Have you been able to decipher the epitaph?"

"No," she answered. "I haven't really tried. I want it to be a mystery. Then I can imagine who is buried here and make up a life story without having to stick to facts."

"That imagination again?" The Judge laughed, but not unkindly. "Well, now that we're here, suppose you show me what happens when you turn the ring."

Elizabeth thought for a moment. "Perhaps you'd better hold my hand, Judge. That way you are sort of in touch with the ring. Just in case there has to be a physical contact for it to work."

"Fine." The Judge took her left hand in his, leaving her little finger free so that the ring wasn't covered. "Well, Bess, let's get on with this adventure. I must say that I'm excited."

She smiled up at him and turned the ring around on her finger. Nothing happened.

Looking into the Judge's questioning eyes, she turned the ring again. And again nothing happened. No sea-sick feeling, no headache, no swirling gray mist, and, most important, no change in time.

"I don't understand it!" She was frantic. "It always works, always. But this time I didn't even feel sick to my stomach!"

The Judge let go of her hand and put his arm around her shoulder. "It's all right, Bess. Don't worry."

"But I am worried! If it doesn't work how can I get to Steve again?" She twisted the ring again and again, wishing with all her heart for the familiar sensations of the change in time, but her stomach stayed calm and the mist and the treeless graveyard with the new tombstones refused to materialize.

"Come on, Bess. Let's go home. There's nothing here, my dear. Nothing but an old graveyard looking just as it has for years. Come." He gently urged her away from the big tree and towards the path.

"I can't go until I've shown you that it *does* work, Judge. I can't go, I can't!"

"Bess, you may have to accept the fact that your mother is right — at least partly. What has happened here today must have shown you that you *have* been imagining things. There is no Steve, Bess. There is no 1870, at least not for Elizabeth Connell of Wells."

"But, Judge.... "

"Come, Bess. Let's go home. Nothing can be gained by staying here. Come on, Bess. Come with me."

Slowly, she followed the Judge out of the cemetery, her thoughts whirling. Why hadn't the change in time worked? Was it because the Judge was with her? Did another person draw off the power of the ring? Would the ring work for her next time, or had she destroyed its power for good? Maybe it was because she had tried to use it in school, away from the spot it should be used? Would she ever see Steve again?

Underneath all these thoughts and questions that scurried around in her mind was one nagging worry. Now the Judge, as well as her mother, would think that she was imagining things. Now she had no way to avoid going to Quesnel to see that psychiatrist on Friday.

91

Chapter 13

Elizabeth's mother was very kind to her the rest of the week, bringing home fresh baking from the restaurant, mending her favourite pair of jeans, and being extremely tolerant of her moods. *It's almost as if she thinks I'm an invalid,* Elizabeth thought. *She's looking after me as if I were sick, or about to burst into tears at any moment.*

And, to tell the truth, tears were never too far away. Elizabeth was confused, upset and worried all at once, and she found that she was missing Steve more than ever. She couldn't believe that he didn't exist; he seemed so real. He had held her and kissed her and laughed with her — how could he not exist? Still, the Judge's visit to the graveyard seemed to prove that Steve was, after all, just a figment of her imagination. She tried to force herself to stop thinking about him. She concentrated on chores and reading, waiting for the rest of the week to pass.

On Friday morning, the day of Elizabeth's appointment with the psychiatrist, Joan Connell was bright and cheerful. "I've got the whole day off work," she announced.

"We'll go into Quesnel early, do some shopping and have a nice lunch before your appointment. We haven't been shopping for ages. I need some new jeans, and let's buy you a pair, too. Maybe we can even manage to get that hair of yours cut."

"No!" Elizabeth was hostile. "I don't want my hair cut." She almost said that Steve liked it the way it was and wanted her to grow it longer, but she held her peace.

"Well, then, all the more time for shopping. Can you think of anything else you need?" Her mother was catering to her, trying to make up for arranging Elizabeth's appointment with the psychiatrist, and for believing that her own daughter was mentally ill. "Anything you need, just say so. I got paid yesterday and I feel rich." She smoothed her hair and smiled nervously. "Anything at all."

"I don't want anything." Elizabeth knew that she was being sullen, but she couldn't help it. She was dreading the appointment with the doctor — psychiatrist! No one in her family had ever seen one, and she had only the faintest idea of how they were supposed to help you. Besides, she didn't *need* help! She was fine and Steve was real and the rest of the world could go hang itself for all she cared!

The morning's shopping expedition was a disaster. Elizabeth was morose and silent, leaving her mother to do all the talking and make all the decisions. Joan Connell chattered on brightly, as if by sheer volume and number of words she could erase Elizabeth's black mood. But nothing worked. They ate pizzas for lunch and, well ahead of the scheduled time, were waiting in Dr. Fendell's office.

It looks just like a regular doctor's office, thought Elizabeth. There were the usual plastic chairs, and tattered magazines, and even a few bright pictures on the walls.

The receptionist seemed surprised that the appointment was for Elizabeth, not for her mother. There was some confusion as they got names and medical insurance numbers straightened out while Elizabeth sat, silent and angry. *That's just great!* she thought. *Now everyone in this room knows that it's me who has to see the psychiatrist.* Then she laughed at herself. *Hey! What are they all doing in this office? They're all seeing him, too.*

Dr. Fendell was a young man, much younger than Elizabeth had imagined he would be. He was clean shaven and had smooth round cheeks that bulged slightly, giving him the look of an elderly baby. His thick blond eyebrows barely showed against his pale skin, and he had a habit of raising them, opening his eyes wide, and saying, "Oh? That's interesting."

Elizabeth didn't like him. But she admitted that she was in a such a foul mood that she wouldn't have liked anyone. She answered all his questions shortly, not saying anything more than she had to. Obviously her mother had spoken to him, for he knew about the change in time and all about Steve. But, for some reason, his questions didn't centre around her experiences in the graveyard.

"Are you fond of your mother?"

"Yes. She's okay."

"How many books do you read a week?"

"Three or four."

"Are you lonely in Wells?"

"Yes, a bit."

"Do you dream a lot?"

"Sometimes."

"Did you ever have an imaginary friend when you were a child?"

At this last question Elizabeth burst out angrily, "Yes! A lot of kids have imaginary friends when they're four or five. But I'm fifteen and Steve isn't imaginary!"

"Oh? That's interesting." He raised his eyebrows and continued with the questions. What did she dream about? Did she have many friends in Vancouver? In Wells? Did she miss her father a great deal? The questions went on and on until finally he stopped, sat back and looked at her.

"Elizabeth, do you want to tell me about Steve?"

The words seemed to come out of her without her even thinking about them. "No! I don't want to tell you anything!"

"Oh?" He was quiet for a few minutes, waiting for her to say something else. "Are you sure you don't want to talk to me? I can't help you very much if I don't know what's worrying you."

Elizabeth sat silently, staring at the floor. She was not normally rude to adults, but she had no wish to tell this baby-faced man *anything* about Steve. Her mother had read it all in her diary; let her mother do the talking.

"Your time is almost up, Elizabeth. I have other patients waiting. Are you sure you don't want to talk to me?"

She shook her head, refusing to answer him. "Oh? That's interesting. . . . Well, let me ask you a few questions that may help you understand what has been happening to you. All right?" This time he waited until she lifted her head and mumbled a reply.

"Your friend, Steve, does he look a lot like your father?"

Elizabeth was puzzled. What did her father have to do with Steve? "No," she said, "he's quite different. He has brown hair and freckles and is tall; Dad is shorter and his hair is the same colour as mine."

"Well, then, does Steve remind you of your father in the way he talks or the way he moves? Or perhaps they both have the same sense of humour?"

"No, not at all." Elizabeth knew that the doctor was trying to make a point, but she couldn't see what it was. "No, they're very different people," she repeated.

"Oh?" The eyebrows went up again. "Well, let me explain what I'm getting at."

I wish you would, thought Elizabeth. She was suddenly nervous, and found her palms beginning to sweat.

"What's your father's name, Elizabeth?" Dr. Fendell asked.

"Mike, Mike Connell," Elizabeth replied, now thoroughly confused.

"No, Elizabeth. His *whole* name."

"I don't see what that has to do with anything!"

"Tell me, Elizabeth."

"Michael," she said, her voice hesitant. "Michael... Steven... Connell."

"Oh? That's *very* interesting." Doctor Fendell lifted his eyebrows and looked at her in silence for a long time.

She sat still, unable to speak. Finally the doctor broke the silence.

"Elizabeth, I want you to think about Steve and your father for a minute. You have missed your father very much these last few months. You and your mother both have told me that. If you look carefully at Steve I think you'll see that he is very much like your dad. I think that your subconscious mind has invented him to take the place of the father you love so much and are missing so desperately."

"No!" Elizabeth stood, her face flushing in anger. "That's sick! Sure I love my father, but not... not *that* way, not the way I love Steve."

"Please sit down Elizabeth. Relax. It's quite normal. A lot of young girls are in love with their fathers, subconsciously, and often they are very jealous of their mothers."

"I won't sit down! You're sick, you and Mom both! Sure, I miss my dad, very much. But I'm not *in love* with him. Steve isn't imaginary; he isn't just a substitute for my Dad."

"Take it easy, now." The doctor stood up, as if he were going to come around the desk to her. "The subconscious mind can —"

"I know what I see! I know what's real. I'm *not* crazy!"

"No one said you were crazy, Elizabeth." Dr. Fendell moved towards her, one hand outstretched. "You're just a very lonely person right now, and your father is very much on your mind. It's understandable that the Steve you see in old Barkerville has the same name as your father. Your subconscious has invented a father figure

97

that you can talk to, touch, love — and not have to share with your mother, because only *you* can see him."

"Bull! If I wanted a father so badly, I've got the Judge. Why would I need to invent Steve?"

"You must realize, Elizabeth," began the doctor, once again moving towards her. "You must understand —"

"No, *you* must understand something. You're a . . . jerk! You don't know what you're talking about!"

"Elizabeth —"

"Stay away from me! The whole idea is ridiculous. It's . . . obscene! It's. . . ." Words failed her. She turned away, leaving the doctor with his hand still outstretched and his mouth open in surprise under the lifted eyebrows, and stormed out of the office.

In the waiting room, her mother looked up, a tentative smile on her face. "Well, dear, how did it —"

"*You* go and talk to him," shouted Elizabeth, her voice high with anger. "The two of you seem to have it all figured out. You're the ones with the sick minds. You go and talk to him!"

Ignoring the stares of the other patients, she grabbed her coat and gloves and left the room, slamming the door behind her.

It's not true, she said to herself as she waited for the elevator. *I didn't invent Steve because I miss my father, because I'm 'in love' with my father. Steve is real, he's real! It's all garbage, sick, stupid garbage.*

The elevator was empty. On the way down to the main floor, she began to cry.

Chapter 14

Joan Connell was horrified by Elizabeth's behaviour in Dr. Fendell's office. At home that night, she let Elizabeth know just how upset she was. "How could the doctor help you if you wouldn't talk to him?" she said. "He said that you were extremely hostile and very rude. He said that you wouldn't confide in him at all, or even listen to his suggestions. I'm very disappointed in you, Elizabeth, and angry, too. I thought you were more mature than that. I guess I was wrong."

Elizabeth kept silent. She would refuse to talk to that doctor again, no matter how many times her mother made her go see him. She'd just sit there and say nothing at all. The idea that Steve was a substitute for her father, that she had invented him because she was lonely, was ridiculous. Sure, she loved her father. But not like that!

"Well, Elizabeth? Can you explain your behaviour?"

"Just leave me alone, Mom. I don't need a doctor's help. I don't need anyone's help."

"But you do need help, Elizabeth, to get over this fixation of yours. There is no Steve and there is no time travelling. The sooner you accept these facts, the sooner you will begin to get well."

"I'm not sick," Elizabeth answered sullenly, then decided against saying anything else. She had no arguments against her mother's logic. The Judge had seen nothing in the graveyard, therefore there was nothing to see. To Joan Connell it was obvious that her daughter was mentally disturbed. Elizabeth chewed on a fingernail and looked down at the floor. No, she couldn't argue. But she would never mention Steve to her mother again.

"The doctor made a suggestion, when he spoke to me after you ran out of the office." Elizabeth's mother took a deep breath, gathering her courage. "Dr. Fendell thinks you will recover from this . . . this illness of yours faster if you stay away from Barkerville, where everything pretends to be in the past."

Elizabeth sat still, waiting. She knew what was coming next.

"So, Margaret Elizabeth, I am forbidding you to go to Barkerville — or the cemetery there. You are not to leave Wells by yourself."

"Come on, Mom. Grounding is for kids. I'm old enough to —"

"And don't try to argue with me, Elizabeth! After your behaviour today, I won't have it. Call it grounding if you like. You may *not* go to Barkerville or the graveyard unless Evan — I mean, the Judge — or I go with you."

Elizabeth realized that there was no point in objecting, no point in saying anything at all. When Joan Connell's face froze into that stern look with the two deep lines between her eyebrows, it meant that she was at the end of her rope, *very* angry, and disagreeing with her or trying to argue would just make it worse. Elizabeth knew it was pointless to try to talk her mother out of her decision right now.

"Promise me, Margaret Elizabeth. Promise me you'll

stay in Wells."

"Okay. I promise." Elizabeth said the words softly and mentally crossed her fingers. She seldom lied to her mother, but she knew that she had no intention of keeping this particular promise. She and Steve had planned to meet on Sunday, December 14, two weeks from now, and she *would* be there to see him, if she had to break every promise she had ever made.

Chapter 15

Resting her skis and poles against a tree, Elizabeth walked through the graveyard gate shortly before two o'clock on Sunday, December 14. It had been two weeks since she had made her promise to her mother, and she had missed Steve more than ever during those weeks. Missed him and worried. What would they do? How could they keep on meeting?

She'd lied to her mother today, told her that she was going over to Janice's house and that the two of them were going skiing on the Jack of Clubs Lake. Her mother was on her way to work, and had smiled happily. "I'm so glad you're making an effort to find a friend, Elizabeth. Have a good time."

Elizabeth was unused to lying. She had felt her cheeks redden, but had turned away quickly and hoped her mother hadn't noticed. *No one should find out,* she thought. Her mother was going to the restaurant and wouldn't be likely to phone Janice's to check up on her. She'd stayed close to home for two Sundays now; her mother probably thought she'd forgotten all about the cemetery and Steve. Sometime this week she'd make a point of going skiing with Janice after school, and maybe even have her over to the trailer for cocoa afterwards. That would please her mother, and ease her own conscience, too.

The weather had warmed up to just below freezing and there hadn't been much new snow since she had come to the graveyard with the Judge. She could see their tracks quite clearly, and she followed them to the grave. Would the ring work this time? When the Judge had been with her nothing had happened, and she hadn't tried the time change since then. What if the Judge's presence had somehow contaminated the ring so that its power to change time was lost?

She sighed and, hoping for the best, turned the ring on her finger. The nausea, the mist, the slight headache — everything happened as it should. Then the mist cleared and she was in the old graveyard, back in 1870, and there was Steve waiting for her.

"Steve, oh, Steve, you're here, you're here!" She ran to him and he gathered her into his arms, holding her close to him for a few minutes. Although she hadn't admitted it to herself she had been worried that her mother and the doctor had been right after all. It wasn't until she actually saw Steve that she realized that a part of her had been doubting his existence for the past few weeks. "You're real, you're solid and you don't look a bit like my dad." Reaching up a hand she gently touched his cheek and laughed at his puzzled expression. "Oh, Steve, you don't know how much I needed to see you!"

"It's been a long time, Bess, very long. I've missed you more than ever."

"I've missed you, too, Steve. And such rotten things have happened that I almost began to think that you weren't real after all!"

"Not real?" He slipped off his gloves and placed his

104

hands on her cheeks. Tilting her head back, he bent down and gently fastened his lips on hers. "There, my little Bess," he said at last. "Was that real enough for you, or should we try it again, just to make sure I *do* exist?" He bent towards her once more, but she laughed and slipped out of his arms.

"Come, let's clear a spot and sit down. I'll get the blanket. Oh, Steve, how did you get up here today? Do your parents know you've come?"

"No." He took the small blanket from her and spread it out in a hollow in the snow. "No, Bess. I lied to them. I said I was going to Marysville to borrow a book from Dr. Black. I've never lied to my parents before and it was hard to do. But I had to see you...." He broke off, turned his head away and coughed, a deep cough that seemed to shake him apart.

"Steve! You're sick!"

"A cough, nothing more. It's been with me for a while now."

Elizabeth took a good look at him. He was so pale that his freckles stood out across his nose as if they'd been painted there. "You don't look well. Are you running a fever? Have you taken your temperature!"

"Temperature?" He looked puzzled. "*My* temperature?"

"Yes. You know, with a thermometer."

"Thermometers are for telling the temperature of the air. We have a big one in the store."

"No! I mean the little ones that doctors use. You know, they tell how high your fever is so they can judge how sick you really are."

"Bess...." Steve sighed, but the end of the sigh turned into another cough. He held his hands to his face until the spasm passed, then said: "I think that's one of those inventions of the future you promised not to talk about. Dr. Black feels your forehead to see if you are feverish."

"I'm sorry." Elizabeth hadn't forgotten her promise not to talk about the future, but in her worry for Steve she hadn't stopped to think what she was saying. Besides, she thought that medical thermometers had been around for hundreds of years. "I'm sorry, Steve, but you don't look well. I was worried and didn't think before I spoke."

"The sickness will pass. Now, come and sit beside me and tell me all the *rotten* things that have happened to you these past weeks. Such things that make you wonder if I am real!"

They sat, nestled into the hollow in the snow, their arms around each other, and Elizabeth told him. She told him how her mother had discovered her diary, of her futile attempt to show the Judge the time change and, finally, of her mother's ban on visits to the graveyard.

Steve sat and listened, trying to muffle his frequent coughing spells. When she finished her story, his arms tightened around her. "Oh, Bess. It *has* been hard on you. Now the both of us are forbidden to come here."

"I lied to my mother, too, Steve. It was hard to do, but I wanted to see you so badly. I had to see you to find out — "

"To find out if I really exist? Yes. I do, and you do too, but the two of us together only exist here, in this one small spot in a graveyard. Oh Bess, if only it could be otherwise!"

He put his head on her shoulder and pressed her face close to his. Even in the cool temperature of the outdoors, his face felt hot. "If only you were from my time. We could go courting together, and you could meet my family and some day, when I become a doctor, we could. . . . "

She looked at him. "We could what, Steve?" she asked softly.

"We could marry, my Bess, and be together always." This time the coughing would not stop easily. His shoulders twisted and he held his hands across his mouth, as if he were trying to push the ugly sound back into his throat.

"Oh, Steve! You *are* sick. You shouldn't have come to the graveyard today."

106

The coughing spell passed; there were tears in Steve's eyes. What had brought them, Elizabeth wondered? The strain of coughing or the words he had just spoken, words that told of a life together that they could never know?

"You must go home, Steve, right away. The cold air will make you worse. Do you have anything to take for your cough? Have you seen the doctor?"

He pulled her to him again. "I'll go soon, Bess, but we have so little time together. Let me stay a while yet. Dr. Black says I should be well in a few days. He has given me a cough elixir which helps some. You worry overmuch."

Elizabeth *was* worried. Her younger brother, Brian, suffered from bouts of bronchitis every winter, and Steve's cough sounded very much like Brian's bronchial one. Brian had to take antibiotics for weeks to get rid of his cough. She knew that there were no antibiotics in Steve's time. A few years ago she had done a report on Sir Alexander Fleming who discovered and named penicillin, the first antibiotic, in 1928. There were no antibiotics for Steve to take.

She knew that bronchitis could become very serious if it wasn't treated properly. That was why her mother worried so much over Brian, pulling him out of minor hockey every winter when he started coughing. Steve would have to get medical help.

"Steve," she said firmly, "there is a medicine that will help you, but your time doesn't have it yet. I'll bring you some; you must take it. But now, go home and go to bed. You need steam in your room to help the cough and you must drink lots of liquids. Also, stay right in bed!"

"My Bess, the doctor." Steve started to laugh, but stopped as he began to cough again. "How will you give me this magic medicine from your time?"

"I'm serious, Steve. Mom has a whole prescription of tetracycline which she brought to Wells just in case one of us got sick and couldn't get into Quesnel to see a doctor. Go home and go to bed. Come back next Sunday. I'll bring you the pills. You *must* take them; they'll stop the cough from turning into something worse, from becoming..."

"Oh, Bess. Of course I'll come next Sunday, sick or well, but only to see you, not for the magic drug with its long name. Drugs from the future might not work on illnesses from the past, you know."

"I'm sure they'll work, Steve. Oh, I wish I could come back before next Sunday, but I can't. Mom is sure to find out if I skip out of school, and it's dark too soon in the afternoons for me to ski up here after three."

"I'll be fine until next Sunday, Bess. Stop worrying about me."

"You will take care, won't you?" They stood, and she shook the snow off the blanket before putting it away in her backpack. "You will stay in bed?"

"Yes, my Bess." He held her hands in both of his. Gently he turned them so the palms faced upwards and planted a soft kiss on each one. "I'll be here, waiting for you and your potion next Sunday, but the sight of you will do me far more good than any tonic you might bring."

He was silent for a moment, then he said, "Next Sunday will be the 21st of December. Only a few days before Christmas. What shall I bring you as a gift, my Bess? What can I bring you that you can take back to your time?"

"Oh, Steve. You've given me your ring. I don't need anything else, except you, healthy and without that awful cough."

"I'll be here, Bess. I'll be here and waiting for you next Sunday."

"Steve? Remember what you were talking about earlier? If... if we were both from the same time?"

"And could go courting and marry and be together always?" His hands tightened around hers. "Yes. I remember."

"I'd like that, Steve. I'd like it very much."

"Bess!" He pulled her to him and she could feel his ribs

108

strain with the effort of suppressing another cough. "I love you, Bess. I love you. Maybe sometime, somehow, your time and my time will come together and you and I. . . . " He stopped and looked into her eyes. "I think it best that I should go home now. Wait Bess, wait until I've gone before you turn the ring. It saddens me so to see you disappear before my very eyes."

"I'll wait. Good-bye, Steve. You will look after yourself, won't you? You will stay in bed?"

"Yes. I'll take care. Good-bye, my dear, my love." He kissed her gently, turned his back and slowly walked out of the graveyard.

Chapter 16

It wasn't until Elizabeth got home that afternoon that she realized that she and Steve hadn't solved their problems at all. Everything remained the same; they were both still forbidden to go to the graveyard. What would they do? Could they continue to sneak away to meet? And how long would it be before her mother discovered that she wasn't skiing with Janice on Sunday afternoons? What would happen when Joan Connell found out that her ban on Elizabeth's visits to the graveyard hadn't been obeyed?

Elizabeth had no answers and neither had Steve. Next Sunday, when she took him the prescription of antibiotics, they would have to talk about it. Maybe by then something would change and they could find a solution to their dilemma.

She and Janice skied after school on Wednesday, then went over to the restaurant for hot chocolate. Joan Connell could hardly contain her pleasure at seeing the two of them together. "Well, Janice, it's so nice to see you again."

Janice mumbled something that could have been a reply and stared intently at the table top.

"I'm so glad you two are getting on well together. Wasn't Sunday a lovely day for skiing? Elizabeth tells me that the two of you had such a good time."

For once, Elizabeth was glad of Janice's awkward shyness. Although she was obviously puzzled by the reference to Sunday, she couldn't gather the courage to say that she hadn't seen Elizabeth at all last week-end.

"Mom, can we have our hot chocolate, please?" Elizabeth said. "It's cold out there, and we're freezing!"

"Sure." Joan Connell bustled away, still smiling, and returned with the steaming mugs and two large orders of french fries as well. "Now don't worry about the calories, girls," she said. "After all that exercise you're entitled to a little extra. Besides, it's on the house."

Elizabeth blushed with embarrassment. Poor Janice had enough trouble with her weight without having all those fattening chips added to her diet. "Really, Mom. . . . " she began, but her mother kept right on talking.

"Come on now, eat up. They won't hurt you a bit. And Janice, I do believe you've lost some weight!"

This time Janice blushed, too. Far from losing, she had gained obviously in the last few months and was painfully aware of it.

"Thanks," she managed to blurt out before reaching for the fries. Mortified by her mother's lack of tact, Elizabeth sat morosely and nibbled at her food. She couldn't find the energy to talk to Janice, and Janice seldom spoke unless someone asked her a question. The trip to the restaurant was a disaster, but Elizabeth wanted her mother to see that Janice was with her.

Now that Mom sees us together, she'll believe me when I tell her that Janice and I are going skiing next Sunday, she thought. *How many times can I get away with this?*

But Joan Connell raised no objections on Sunday when Elizabeth announced that she and Janice were going skiing. "It's good for you to have a friend, Elizabeth, even if Janice is a less-than-fascinating conversationalist. Go ahead and have a good time."

An hour later, with the stolen bottle of tetracycline in her jacket pocket and her skis and poles resting against a tree by the graveyard gate, Elizabeth followed the footprints that led to her special spot in the cemetery. (She was now a fairly accomplished skier and could manage the long uphill climb of the graveyard trail with her skis on.)

Checking to make sure that she still had the pills, she turned the ring, shut her eyes momentarily while the sick feeling passed, and then was back in the old 1870 cemetery.

Steve was not there.

Puzzled, she looked around for him. He had never been late before. Usually he was there well before two o'clock and was waiting for her when she emerged from her time. But today the graveyard was empty except for the usual collection of chickadees who were scolding her noisily for disturbing them.

She spread the small thermal blanket in the hollow of snow that Steve had scooped out the week before, sat down, and waited. The graveyard was deserted, but in the distance she could hear an occasional sound drifting up from Barkerville. The chickadees hopped and fluttered from bush to bush, scattering small clumps of snow from the branches as they did so. Although it was warm, just below freezing, the sky was overcast. The shortened tombstones with their lopsided caps of snow cast no shadows, but seemed to fade into the bleak landscape until they were nothing more than unidentifiable grey lumps.

She waited. Steve did not arrive. She checked her watch. It was after three. Perhaps he wasn't coming today. But he promised to meet her, promised to try her 'magic medicine from the future' even though he'd teased her gently about it.

113

Maybe she had the wrong day? No, she'd said she'd be back in one week. Today was Sunday, December 21. It was the right day.

She stood up. He wasn't coming, and she might as well go home. It would begin to get dark soon, and she had to get home before the light faded entirely. She should leave now and come back next Sunday.

As she was about to turn the ring, a horrible thought occurred to her. Perhaps Steve was too ill to come today. He'd been coughing dreadfully last Sunday; maybe he'd become worse during the week. If only he'd managed to get to the cemetery so she could have given him the pills!

But, if Steve were too sick to come to her, to get the medicine that would help him, then he must be *very* ill. He had promised to be here today, and he badly needed the antibiotic. If he couldn't come to her, then she would have to go to him.

She was frightened. The only other time she had tried to leave the graveyard she had almost disappeared. What would happen if she went all the way into Barkerville? Would she disappear entirely? And, if she didn't disappear, what would happen if someone else saw her? With her short ski trousers, thick wool socks, and oddly shaped boots she didn't look as if she belonged in Barkerville in 1870.

Elizabeth thought hard. It was beginning to get dark. She would have to make up her mind — either return home right now, or go into Barkerville, try to find Steve's home and give him the tetracycline.

Then she decided. As much as it frightened her, she would have to find Steve. Taking a deep breath, she left the graveyard and started down the trail to Barkerville.

The trail seemed wider than it was in 1980, and the snow had been packed down so that walking was easier. She met no one all the way down the hill. By the time she reached the bottom of the graveyard trail and turned towards the town, she could not see her hands, or her feet, or any part of her body.

Although she had been expecting this, it was still frightening. Nervously, she had watched her body become more and more transparent, until it disappeared entirely. Not seeing her feet bothered her more than anything else. They were there because she could feel them, feel the crisp snow beneath the soles of her boots. But when she looked down she could see only the packed snow. After she stumbled once or twice, she decided not to look down at all. Her feet were there and were quite capable of carrying her without being checked on every few seconds.

She left no footprints, cast no shadow, but she was there. She could feel her face, her hands, the texture of her jacket, but she couldn't see herself. Except for the ring. It floated along beside her, real and solid and in no way ghostlike. She knew it wasn't really floating; she could feel it on her hand, but not being able to see her hand made the ring look as if it were suspended in thin air, moving jerkily along as she swung her arms.

I guess the ring truly belongs to both times, she thought. *Because it's a part of 1870, it hasn't disappeared. I'm not part of this time — neither are my clothes — so we just aren't here. Perhaps it's a way of making sure that I can't do any harm to the past or change anything that might affect the future.*

Then an upsetting thought struck her. The only other time she had left the graveyard, Steve had tried to take her nearly invisible hand to help her back up the trail. He hadn't been able to do it. His hand had passed right through hers as if she were a reflection in a pool of water. If he hadn't been able to feel *her,* would he be able to see, to touch and swallow the pills she had brought?

She pulled the bottle of tetracycline capsules out of her pocket. She could hear them rattling around in their plastic container, she could feel the container in her hand, but when she brought it up in front of her eyes she could see nothing.

The pills were from the future, too, and had no place in old Barkerville. Steve would not be able to see them — or

115

swallow them. They would do him no more good than a mouthful of air.

Oh, no! They're useless. Useless! I can't help him at all! Angrily, she threw the bottle away. She heard the pills rattle as the bottle tumbled through the air, and waited for the sound of the invisible container hitting the ground.

She heard nothing. Puzzled, she kicked at the snow where the bottle should have landed. There was nothing there, nothing at all.

Oh, great! This is ridiculous! Invisible pills that disappear in mid-air — wouldn't Dr. Fendell love that! I wonder how he'd explain it — my subconscious mind again!

She walked on, wondering what had happened to the pills. She had felt them in her hand, but when she threw them they vanished. *Maybe they went back to 1980. I know it's the ring that pulls me through time. Maybe once the pills lost contact with me and with the ring, they went back into the future. I'll look for them on my way home.*

But she couldn't do that. It was getting darker every minute. She wouldn't be able to see the trail on her way back. How would she manage skiing the eight kilometers home in the dark?

Well, she couldn't worry about that now. Having come this far, having almost adjusted herself to the weird sensation of being invisible, she was going to go on — on to Barkerville and Steve. The antibiotic couldn't help him, but she had to see him, just to make sure he was all right. When she wasn't back by dinner time her mother would get hold of Janice and find out that they hadn't been skiing together. Then she'd know where Elizabeth was, and would either come to the graveyard herself or send the Judge to bring her home. All she had to do was to get back to the cemetery, and someone would be there waiting to take her home.

It wouldn't be pleasant. She had lied and broken promises and now her mother would do a much more thorough

116

job of grounding her, but she *had* to see Steve. At least for a little while. And she wouldn't worry about what happened afterwards.

Ahead of her she could see Barkerville. She touched her face, making sure that she was still solid, at least to herself, and walked into the old town.

Chapter 17

Saint Saviour's church loomed up ahead of her, standing guard over the town just as it did in 1980. The tall steeple and high arched windows bore a fresh coat of white paint which stood out starkly in the early dusk.

It looks so new, she thought. *It can't be any more than a year old. I wonder what it looks like inside.* She shook her head, and hurried on past the church. There was no time to go in right now. Another time, perhaps, she'd come back and explore the Barkerville of 1870. Right now, though, she had to keep going.

The main street of Barkerville looked much the same as it did in 1980, but some of the familiar buildings were missing. *I suppose they haven't been re-built yet after the Great Fire of 1868. And look at all the saloons! There must be twenty of them!*

She noticed that the Kelly Hotel was missing and so was the small one-room school house. But down the road she recognized the Theatre Royal, and the new fire alarm bell already in place on its tall steeple, ready to sound in the event of another great fire.

She passed the Wake-Up Jake and smiled to herself. They certainly didn't serve cokes and milkshakes there now, just hearty meals for Barkerville's residents.

The main road seemed to be in terrible condition, much worse than modern Barkerville's road. Even under the layer of packed snow, she could see the large ruts and potholes threatening to break the legs of pedestrians and horses alike. *It looks as if no one bothers to repair the streets at all*, she thought. *I think I'll try the boardwalk.*

The boardwalks, the raised sidewalks that were a feature of modern Barkerville, were just as important in old Barkerville. The Judge had told her that the sidewalks and buildings in the town were raised for a very simple reason: Williams Creek had a habit of flooding its banks and pouring into the town once in a while. But it looked as if every store owner on the main street had constructed his building and boardwalk without considering the heights of those on either side. No two were the same height off the ground; uneven steps led up and down from one walkway to another. She smiled to herself as she thought of the problems this must cause the patrons of the town's many saloons.

Elizabeth knew where she was going. Steve had told her that the store his family owned was in the centre of town, on the main street, and that their home was directly behind it. She could already see the sign, Baker's Emporium, ahead of her. Now she had to find an alleyway that led off the main street to the houses behind.

The sound of voices startled her. Two men in tall hats and long black coats stood talking on the walkway, almost directly in front of her. They must have come out of one of the hotels or saloons. So far she had seen no one else. Barkerville seemed deserted this early Sunday evening, and she had assumed that the dinner hour had drawn everyone inside.

Although she knew that the men could not see her, she worried that she might not be able to get past them.

Would she be discovered? Or would she be pushed off the narrow boardwalk? *I may be invisible,* she thought, *but I don't want to risk a fall from this height. My bones would probably break just as easily as they would in my own time.*

She edged closer to the buildings. Perhaps, if she stayed right by the wall, she could get by the two men safely. She hoped that no one would choose that moment to emerge from a doorway beside her, forcing her away from the safety of the wall. Although she was pretty sure that a person would pass right through her, it was a feeling she didn't particularly want to experience.

One hand on the buildings beside her, she moved slowly towards the two men, keeping as close to the storefronts as possible. The wall was solid; she could feel the rough texture of the wood with her hand. Obviously she couldn't just glide through walls like a real ghost. She had to obey the laws of her own time and enter houses through doors, climb stairs, and be careful not to fall off the boardwalks.

People can't see me or touch me, but the ground and the buildings feel solid and real. What kind of a ghost am I, anyway? She promised herself that she would think this whole thing through later.

She was closer to the men now, creeping slowly along the front of the stores. They laughed, and she jumped at the sudden noise.

"Yes, Your Honour, I'll make sure that those arrangements are completed before your next visit. You can depend on it." Shaking hands, the two men separated; the one called 'Your Honour' turned and began to walk directly towards her.

It was Judge Begbie! Elizabeth stood still and stared. He looked just like Evan — the tall, upright stature, the carefully trimmed and waxed moustache, and the grey beard with the distinctive streak of black down the centre. It could be Evan himself standing in front of her.

She pressed herself closer to the wall as he moved towards her. *Hey, Judge!* she thought. *If I called out, could you hear me? What would you think if a voice from nowhere suddenly wished you a good evening?* She giggled, putting her hands in front of her mouth. She wasn't sure if anyone from 1870 could hear her, or if her voice was as insubstantial as her body, but she wasn't taking any chances.

Judge Begbie stopped in front of her, a puzzled expression on his face. He rubbed his hand over his eyes then stared directly at her. *But he can't see me*, she thought. *What is he looking at?*

The Judge reached out a hand towards her. Elizabeth couldn't understand what he was doing. What could he see? She looked down. She couldn't see her hands, but she knew they were in front of her face. The gold ring! It floated in front of her, clearly visible in the fading light.

Hurriedly, she pulled her hands away from her face, watching Judge Begbie's eyes follow the ring's movement. She thrust her hands behind her back, but the Judge's eyes still followed the ring.

Of course, she realized. *He can see it right through me. I'm not hiding it at all!*

Again Judge Begbie reached out his hand, stretching it towards the ring. Elizabeth panicked. If he pulled it off her invisible hand, how would she get back to her own time? Would she suddenly be drawn there, as the tetracycline pills seemed to have been, or would she stay in 1870 forever — an insubstantial ghost trapped in the wrong time?

She looked behind her. A large wooden barrel stood by the door of the hotel she had just passed. It probably held water in case of fire, but right now it was empty. Quickly, she stepped back towards it, watching Judge Begbie as he, too, began to move. She slipped her hand behind the barrel, using it to screen the ring from his sight.

The Judge stopped and again rubbed his hand across his face. He blinked his eyes and shook his head slowly. "I thought I saw . . . ," he began, then he turned away. "Perhaps I'm in need of a tonic," he said as he walked past her. "A tonic — or something stronger. Yes, definitely this calls for something stronger." He hurried away down the boardwalk.

Elizabeth knew of Judge Begbie's liking for 'strong spirits' and she had no doubt what the 'something stronger' would be. *Poor Judge,* she thought. *You'll puzzle over this for years, wondering if you actually saw a gold ring appear and disappear before your eyes. When I get back home I'll ask my Judge if he has ever read anything about Judge Begbie seeing apparitions.*

It was almost completely dark by now, and she made her way cautiously along the uneven planking. Spotting a small alleyway that led between two stores, she climbed down to it. This would take her to the street behind Baker's Emporium, to Steve's house.

The sound of voices reached her as she turned the corner. A small woman, Steve's mother, was standing in front of one of the houses, talking to a bearded man who carried a small black bag. She had found Steve's home.

"Thank you for coming, doctor." The voices carried easily in the cold air. "We've been so concerned."

"He'll be all right, Mrs. Baker. Just make sure he stays warm and quiet, and give him that medicine in a few hours. I'll be back later tonight to check on him. Good evening."

The doctor turned to go. Steve's mother stood watching him as he made his way down the path to the street, and Elizabeth took advantage of the moment to slip through the open door of the house. Now she wouldn't have to risk someone seeing the front door open, apparently all by itself, when she went in. Pressing herself against the wall, she waited until the woman walked past her. She hoped that Steve's mother would lead her directly to his room.

Mrs. Baker walked down the hallway and paused before a closed door. She sighed and tidied a stray lock of blonde hair that had escaped from its tight bun. Then, straightening her shoulders and fixing a smile on her face, she pushed open the door and went into the room. Elizabeth followed, thankful that the ring hadn't been noticed in the dim, lamplit hall.

"Steven? Steven, are you awake?" His mother spoke softly; her voice trembled slightly.

"Mother?" Steve's voice was weak. He lay on a bed in the middle of the room. Beside him a large brass bucket full of hot water threw a faint mist into the air. He was pale, even paler than he'd been on the Sunday before.

His mother bent over the bed and touched his cheek. "Dr. Black says you'll be all right, son. He will be back later to see how you are. Sleep now, and I'll bring you your medicine in a while."

"What time is it?" Steve struggled to sit up, his body twisting with a cough as he did so. "What time is it, Mother?"

"It is after dark, son. Nearly five o'clock. Lie back, now, and rest. Sleep if you can, or would you rather I sat and read to you?"

"It's too late, then. She will have gone home. I've missed her, and I promised to be there. Oh, Mother, I should have gone outside today, for a short walk. I'm sure the fresh air would have helped me."

"Now, Steven, don't start that nonsense again. As sick as you are, you are not going anywhere for a few days. I do not understand why, suddenly today, you began insisting that you go outside."

"It is Sunday, isn't it?"

"Yes, son. It's Sunday, December 21, and we want you to be well by Christmas. You must stop worrying and rest. Sleep, Steven. It's nature's way of healing."

Pushing him gently back onto the bed, she drew the covers up around him, kissed him on the forehead and left, closing the door behind her. Elizabeth was alone with Steve.

124

Quickly she moved to his bedside. "Steve, Steve, can you hear me?"

Steve's eyes opened and he looked around the room. "Bess?" he said, puzzled, "Bess?"

"I'm here, Steve, I'm here! I'm right beside you."

"Bess?" he said again, "I can't see you."

Elizabeth held up her left hand. The ring glowed in the light from the small lamp beside the bed. "Look, Steve. You can see the ring. I'm here!"

His eyes widened as the ring seemed to float in front of his face. "Oh, Bess! You came to find me when I couldn't come to the graveyard to see you."

"I was worried, Steve, when you weren't there. I had to make sure you were all right. You *are* going to be all right, aren't you? You *are* getting better?"

Steve tried to laugh, but stopped as he began to cough. "The doctor says it will pass. Don't worry. But I'm as weak as a new-born kitten."

She put her hand on his cheek. "You're so warm, Steve. You must have a high fever. Can you feel my hand?"

"No." He smiled. "Only the ring. It feels cool against my face. But I can hear you, Bess, and I know that you are with me. I wish I could see you — " He coughed. The cough sounded different: deeper and drier. He seemed to have barely enough energy to raise his hand to cover his mouth.

"Oh, Steve. You're sick, very sick!"

"I have a strong constitution, Bess. I'll recover. Did you bring me the magic medicine from the future?"

"No. I tried to, but it disappeared once I left the grave-yard. It doesn't belong in your time and it couldn't have done you any good." She sat down on the edge of the bed, resting her hand on his pillow. She told him how she had gradually faded away, all except the ring, and of her walk through his Barkerville. He laughed at her story of the meeting with Judge Begbie.

"Oh, Bess, he's a stubborn man. He doesn't believe in

ghosts — not even ghost rings!" They both laughed, Steve trying to hold back a cough.

"Steven!" The door swung open. His mother stood there, silhouetted against the light from the hall. "Steven, I heard voices. Is someone with you? What is the matter, son?"

Steve tried to sit up, but fell back on the pillow. "I was.... I was thinking. I must have been talking out loud."

"I thought I heard another voice. And laughter." She came to his bedside and Elizabeth quickly moved to the foot of the bed. "You are flushed, son. Perhaps I should call Dr. Black. You must have been dreaming, or having hallucinations."

"No, Mother. I'm all right."

Elizabeth sat down carefully on the foot of the bed, her left hand resting on the thick quilt. Steve's mother stood beside the bed, her face drawn with lines of tension. She looked down towards the foot of the bed and her face suddenly lit up.

"Steven! That's Amy's ring! Where did you find it, son? I thought it was lost forever." Bending down, she reached out to pick up the ring.

Elizabeth sat still, too frightened to move. She had forgotten about the ring being visible. Now, if she took her hand away, Steve's mother would see it move. But if she left her hand where it was, the ring would be pulled from her finger.

"Ring?" With a great effort Steve sat up, moving his feet as he did so. Taking advantage of the motion of the blankets, Elizabeth slipped her hand down behind the bed, hiding the ring from view.

Steve grabbed at the blankets by his feet, closing his hand as if he had picked something up. "Yes. I want to keep it under my pillow, Mother. It comforts me." He lay back down and slipped his hand under his pillow.

"I'm glad you found the ring, Steven."

"I am, too, Mother. Very glad. Now. . . now I would like to sleep."

"Are you sure you wouldn't like me to stay with you, son? Would you like to talk?"

"No, Mother. But thank you. I think I'll sleep now." Again a cough shook him. "I seem to cough less when I sleep."

"Very well, then. I'll be back in a while. Call for me if you need anything or. . . ." She smiled, and left the room.

"Bess?" Steve whispered. "Bess, where are you?"

Elizabeth sat beside him, placing the ring on the pillow so that he could see it by turning his head slightly. "I'm still here, Steve. Right beside you."

"Oh, Bess, I feel so weak. I have to sleep. Will you stay with me for a little while? Sit there and be with me? Soon I'll be stronger and we can talk again, but my voice fails me right now. Stay with me, Bess."

"I'll stay, Steve. I'll stay." She touched a lock of hair that had fallen over his forehead, amazed that she could feel him while her touch was no more than empty air to him.

"My Bess. My love. Stay with me. Don't leave. Stay. . . ."

His eyes were shut, the thick lashes lying against his cheeks. His breathing was ragged: a long deep breath followed by a series of short, panting ones. Elizabeth settled down to wait.

Chapter 18

It was warm in the room, and the steam from the brass bucket hung around the lamp like a halo. Elizabeth sat beside Steve, waiting while he slept. He seemed to grow paler as she watched him, and his breathing became more laboured. Once he muttered something and she bent her head to listen, but the words were faint and garbled, making no sense to her. She sat watching him, while time passed slowly.

Mrs. Baker came in and Elizabeth quickly moved around the bed, to the side away from the door. She slipped her hand under Steve's pillow, hiding the ring from sight, as the small woman stood silently, looking down at her son.

"Steven," Mrs. Baker called at last. "Steven, I have brought you the medicine Doctor Black left."

"Mother?" Steve opened his eyes. "Mother, is Bess still here?"

"Bess?" Her voice was tense. "There's no one here now, Steven. You must have been dreaming." She slipped one arm behind his shoulders, helping him to sit up. "Here. Drink this. The doctor says it will help you."

Steve obediently drank the glass of darkish liquid, then eased himself back onto the pillow.

"You have been sleeping, son. Do you feel any better?"

"Yes, somewhat. I think I could sleep again, Mother. I'm so weak and I feel light-headed."

"I'll bring you some more hot water, Steven, then you can sleep again." She picked up the bucket and made her way to the door, closing it behind her.

"Bess? Bess?" Steve whispered. "Are you still here?"

"Yes, Steve." Elizabeth slipped her hand out from under the pillow and held it so he could see the ring. "I'm right beside you, right here."

"It's late. Will your mother be concerned about you?"

"It'll be okay, Steve. I'll make up some excuse."

Mrs. Baker returned with the steaming brass bucket and placed it beside the bed. "This notion of yours that steam helps your cough, Steven. . . . Well, Doctor Black said that it can't do any harm, and it seems to comfort you. Although where you got the notion that steam is therapeutic, I don't know."

Elizabeth smiled, wondering how Steve would answer that one. She had been the one who told him to use steam.

"A friend, Mother. A friend told me."

His mother bent over him again and straightened the covers. "Amy's ring," she said, as she caught sight of it on the pillow. Elizabeth had forgotten to hide it this time. "Are you sure you don't want me to put it on the dresser for you? It would be safer there."

"No!" Steve placed his hand gently over Elizabeth's, hiding the ring from view. "I want it here, beside me. Don't take it away."

"Of course not, son, if it pleases you to have it close. Keep it by you."

She felt his forehead. "You are still feverish. Perhaps the medicine will help. Can I bring you something to eat?

I have made a soup and it's hot and ready. . . ."

"No, Mother. I'm not hungry. Perhaps later. . . ." Steve closed his eyes. His mother stood looking down at him, her face tense and worried. "Sleep now, Steven. The doctor will be here in a while. You will be well soon. You *will* be well."

She sighed, then turned to go. "Call me if you need anything, please."

The door closed behind her. Steve opened his eyes. "Bess? Oh, Bess, I feel so strange. Are you really there?"

"Of course I am. You can hear me, can't you?"

"Will you stay for a while longer? I slept so soundly just now, knowing you were with me. Please stay. . . ." His voice trailed off as his eyes closed.

"Yes, I'll stay," Elizabeth began, then realized that he was asleep again. Settling herself more comfortably on the edge of the bed, she looked down at him. She was worried. Steve was so ill. Although his cough had eased, his fever appeared to be going up and he seemed to be getting weaker. If only she had been able to bring him the antibiotic! If only he had lived in her time where modern medicine was available and modern doctors could look after him. If only . . . if only she could help somehow, not just sit here, silent and invisible, while he got sicker and sicker.

The house was quiet. Elizabeth wondered briefly where Steve's father was. She hadn't seen him yet, and she was curious to know if he looked like his son. She sat, listening, starting at the occasional sound, and watching the little wraiths of steam circle the lamp. Steve stirred once, and a small moan escaped from his lips. She felt so helpless, sitting on the bed, unable to do anything.

She sat, she waited. How long she wasn't sure. Although she was wearing her watch, she could not read it. It was as invisible as the rest of her. *It must be late*, she thought. *After midnight!* It had been early evening when she found Steve, and she had been here a long time. Her mother would be frantic by now. Joan Connell had probably come to Barkerville to look for her, maybe even passed close by, but a hundred years in the future.

No! I shouldn't think about that now, she told herself. *It seems to help Steve to know that I'm here, and I'll stay with him for as long as he needs me.*

After a long period of silence, voices echoed in the hallway. The doctor had come back, and he and Mrs. Baker were coming to Steve's room. Elizabeth slipped her hand under the pillow again, hoping that no one would come around to her side of the bed.

Dr. Black looked concerned as he checked Steve. "The fever must break soon," he said. "Then he will begin to recover."

Steve was still asleep. Once, his eyes opened briefly, then shut again, and his head rolled slackly on the pillow.

"Has he been like this for long?" the doctor asked.

"For several hours, doctor," replied Mrs. Baker. "And . . . and he has been talking to himself, too. He calls for someone named Bess."

The doctor stood up. "If the fever breaks soon he will be fine," he said. "I can do no more for him right now. But he's a strong boy, Mrs. Baker, and he's giving the sickness a brave fight." He turned to look at Steve again.

"Bess?" Steve's voice was low, but there was no mistaking what he was saying. "Bess? Where are you?"

"Doctor, do you hear? I stood outside this room earlier and listened to him talk to this Bess. I fear for his mind, doctor, I fear for his mind!"

"It's the fever, that's all. His mind is sound, but his brain is clouded by the heat of his body."

Both of them turned to leave the room, Mrs. Baker with one hand on the doctor's arm, seeking his reassurance. "I will stay with him, then," Elizabeth heard her say as they left. "I will stay right by his side until the fever breaks."

Then they were gone. Steve opened his eyes and called her name again. "I'm here, Steve, I'm here," she whispered.

"I heard my Mother, Bess. She's going to sit with me.... She will stay throughout the night, as she did last night." He sighed. "You must go now. I can't talk to you with my mother so close. I become confused. I forget which of you I am talking to. You must...." His voice faded, but with an effort he finished the sentence. "You must go, my Bess, my love."

"Oh, Steve, I can't leave you when you're so sick."

"Bess, you can't help me. Your medicine... your touch... all of you... all from the future. From your time. No help in my time." His eyes closed again.

"No. I'll stay. I want to stay, Steve."

Steve pushed himself slowly up into a sitting position. "Bess. Look. I feel stronger... stronger. Go now, Bess. The cough has abated. I feel better. Come to the graveyard next Sunday. I will be there, and we'll be together in our own place again. Go home now, Bess. Go to your own time. Go...."

The effort of speaking tired him and he lay back on the pillow. "Smile for me once, Bess. I can't see it, but I will know if you smile. Then go home and wait for me. All will be well."

Elizabeth smiled, but tears were gathering in her eyes. She knew Steve was right. She couldn't help him, and, with his mother planning to spend the rest of the night by his side, she couldn't even talk to him. The best thing to do would be to go home and try to straighten out the mess that her disappearance must have created. But she didn't want to go. Steve said that he was feeling better, but she wasn't convinced. He looked so ill.

"Bess? I hear my mother coming...." Elizabeth, too, could hear footsteps in the hall.

Quickly, she made up her mind. "Yes, Steve, I hear. I'm going now, but I'll be in the graveyard next Sunday, no matter what. I promise. And if you're too sick to come there, I'll come to you again. Oh, Steve...."

She kissed him, feeling his hot, dry lips against hers. He smiled, almost as if he could feel her kiss. "Goodbye,

Steve. Please, please get well."

"Oh, my Bess. I *will* be well and everything will be as it was. Next Sunday, Bess. Next Sunday."

"Yes. Next Sunday. Goodbye, Steve. Goodbye." She hurried to the door. Mrs. Baker was coming into the room, and Elizabeth slipped past her and out the door.

"Steven? Steven, were you calling for me?" The door closed behind her, and Elizabeth was alone in the hall. She would have to risk opening the front door and slipping out, hoping that no one would choose that moment to come into the hallway. Reaching for the doorknob, she stopped. Steve's voice, faint but clear, came through the closed bedroom door.

"Goodbye, Bess. I love you! I love you!"

Oh, your poor mother, Steve, Elizabeth thought as she listened to the murmur of voices. Mrs. Baker was probably trying to calm her hallucinating son. Then she opened the door and went quietly out into the night.

Chapter 19

The clouds had lifted and a large moon hung low in the sky, lighting up the town almost as if it were daylight. Elizabeth had no difficulty finding her way back to the main street and along it, to the graveyard trail. She met no one. Barkerville slept, silent and lonely under the full moon. She talked to herself as she walked. "He *did* seem a bit stronger. He'll be all right, he *will!* He'll be fine by next Sunday and we'll meet in the graveyard, somehow, and everything will be the way it should be."

Still talking reassuringly to herself, she finished the steep climb and entered the cemetery.

Elizabeth had never been here at night before, and, although she thought she had lost all fear of the place, it made her nervous tonight. The bright moon lit up the snow and the tombstones cast strange, deep shadows. The chickadees had long since gone to sleep, and the silence was total. She shivered, and made her way quickly to the spot where the ring would pull her back to her own time. The sooner she got out of here, away from the ancient shadows and the silence, and back to her own time, the happier she would be. Even if it did mean facing an angry and upset mother. She turned the ring.

"Bess!" The voice spoke from behind her, and she jumped, as frightened as she'd been the first time Steve had spoken to her. "Bess! I've been waiting for you." The Judge stood behind the grave.

"Oh, Judge!" Elizabeth ran to him and he put his arms around her. "Oh, Judge, he's so sick. . . ." Then she began to cry, letting out all the tears and the tension that had been building up in her over the long night.

"Easy, Bess, easy." The Judge held her firmly, letting her cry against his shoulder. "I know it's been hard on you. I knew that something must have happened to your Steve or you wouldn't have been gone so long. Take it easy and tell me about it."

She raised her tear streaked face. "Judge? You sound as if you *do* believe me, about the time change and Steve?"

"I've been waiting for you right here, Bess, for three hours. One minute I saw nothing, and the next minute you stood in front of me. An experience like that tends to make a believer out of one. I know that you were somewhere where I couldn't see you. And now you have come back, and we must go and face your mother."

"Is she . . . ?" began Elizabeth.

"Very much so," answered the Judge. "When you didn't come to the restaurant for dinner she phoned Janice's house and found out you weren't there. We all knew where you had gone."

"I had to go, Judge. He was sick, and then when he didn't come to the graveyard I knew he was worse. I tried to take him some medicine, but—"

"Yes, I know. I found your mother's prescription bottle on the trail, Bess. The others went into Barkerville to look for you, after we checked the highway from Wells. I knew you would return to the graveyard if you could, and

I came here to wait."

"The others? What others?"

"Your mother is here, looking for you, and so is Mr. MacDonald and two men who are staying at the hotel. It's after three, Bess. You've been missing for over twelve hours! Everyone has been worried. We were afraid that you had fallen while you were skiing and were lying alone in the snow, hurt and unable to move. People die from exposure after only a few hours in this temperature, you know."

Suddenly, Elizabeth noticed the cold. She could feel the tears on her cheeks beginning to freeze, and was conscious that her toes and fingers were cold.

"Come, Bess. I have a thermos of coffee in the car. Let's get down to the parking lot so I can tell the others that you're safe. Then we can call off the search."

The Judge picked up Elizabeth's skis and they started down the trail. As they walked, she told him everything: of how she had lied to her mother, her worries about Steve, her journey through 1870 Barkerville, and sitting ghost-like by Steve's bed, waiting and hoping. The Judge laughed when she said that she had seen the real Judge Begbie and that the two of them really did look alike.

"Why, then, I'm flattered. I've always thought that the real Judge Begbie was a striking figure of a man."

In the parking lot, the Judge started the car, handed Elizabeth a thermos of coffee, and began to honk the horn. Three long blasts followed by silence, then three long blasts again. "That's the signal if you're found and you're well," he said. "Sound carries a long way in this cold air, and the others will be coming out of Barkerville any time now."

Soon Elizabeth could hear voices and recognized the loudest and angriest among them as her mother's. "Margaret Elizabeth Connell! Where have you been?"

Elizabeth took a deep breath and shivered. Her mother

sounded furious. *It's a good thing I'm too old to be spanked,* she thought. *Or am I? Maybe a good, honest spanking would be better than what is going to happen to me now.*

Chapter 20

In spite of Elizabeth's fears, her mother said nothing more
to her on the way back to Wells. Even when they were
home and she tried to offer an excuse, Joan Connell
tightened her lips and said, "We won't talk about it now,
Elizabeth. Go to bed. School is out for the holidays, so
you can sleep late. Go to bed."

And that was that! Elizabeth was relieved that the
outburst she had expected from her mother hadn't
occurred, though she felt some apprehension about what
would happen tomorrow morning. But at four o'clock in
the morning, she was too tired to worry about it. She fell
into a dreamless sleep.

She woke up about one in the afternoon to the sound of
a deep voice calling her name. "Elizabeth. Time to wake
up, sleeping beauty!"

For a moment she thought that it was Steve's voice, and
she sat up in astonishment. But it was her father who sat
on the edge of the bed, smiling down at her.

"Dad! What are you doing here? Oh, Dad!" She threw

herself into his arms, and he held her tightly. "I'm so glad you've come, Dad. Mom is so angry at me. I lied to her and disobeyed her but —"

"Your mother's not angry, Elizabeth. But she's very upset. You gave her quite a scare last night. She phoned me as soon as she realized that you were missing. Brian and I flew in on the morning plane, and your friend, the Judge, picked us up in Quesnel. We're staying for Christmas."

Elizabeth felt ashamed. "Mom didn't need to call you. I'm all right." She hesitated, then said, "I suppose she's told you everything? About the graveyard and. . . ."

"And Steve." Mike Connell's voice was gentle. "Yes. I've known ever since she read your diary, Elizabeth. I've been worried about you, too."

"Dad, *you* don't think I'm crazy, do you? You don't believe that I'm seeing things that don't exist?"

"I don't know what to believe, Elizabeth. I think that you've been lonely, and I know that this little town must be a strange place to live in. But you don't have to worry about it any more. It's over."

"Over? What do you mean? Steve is sick and I have to go back and see him next Sunday and —"

"You're going home, Elizabeth! Your mother and I have talked about it. Both of you are coming home. She has to work until after Christmas, but you're flying home next Sunday evening."

His smile was broad as he hugged her. "I've missed you both. I'm so glad your mother has decided to come back to Vancouver."

"She can't leave *now!*" Elizabeth was horrified. The last thing in the world she wanted to do was leave Wells, and Steve. "Mom's signed a contract. She has to stay for a year."

"The MacDonalds understand, Elizabeth. They've released her from the contract. The new cook will be here next Monday to take over."

140

"Understand? What exactly do they understand?" Elizabeth thought she knew the answer to that question, but she felt she had to ask it anyway. Mike Connell brushed a strand of hair away from his face and sighed. His eyes were kind, but she could tell that he had been under a strain.

"They understand that you're not well, Elizabeth. They understand that the best thing for you is to be as far away from Barkerville as possible — and as soon as possible. That's what Dr. Fendell recommended weeks ago, and your mother is blaming herself for not taking his advice immediately."

"But she can't leave just because of some dumb psychiatrist's —"

"Elizabeth, it's not just because of you. Your mother wants to come home. She wants to come back to me and Brian. Whatever it was she needed to find in Wells, she's found it, and she's ready to come back to Vancouver. You've given her an excuse for leaving earlier, that's all."

"Really? She *wants* to go back? She's not talking about a divorce anymore?" Elizabeth's eyes widened at the news. But she didn't want to leave Barkerville, and Steve. Three months ago all she wanted to do was go home, but not now. "But Dad, I don't want people to think that Mom's leaving because I'm crazy."

"No one thinks that, Elizabeth. They all realize how alone you've been these past five months. No one thinks you're really *crazy*, just young and lonely and missing your family and your own home."

Elizabeth pushed her hair behind her ears and sat up straight. "I don't want to go," she said.

"Oh." Her father looked at her steadily. "I want very much to have you home again, both you and your mother. Besides, Elizabeth, you're not even sixteen years old. Do you really have any choice in the matter?"

"No. I guess I don't," Elizabeth said in a small voice. She felt very confused. Part of her wanted to go home again,

141

another part desperately wanted to stay in Wells. She was angry at her mother for using her 'illness' as an excuse to return to Vancouver, yet she was relieved that her parents had reconciled their differences and that the family would be together again.

"I know how you feel, Elizabeth, but believe me it's the best thing for all of us. Now, come on and get dressed and we'll go over to the restaurant for lunch — although I guess *you* can call it breakfast. Brian is already over there, sampling your mother's french fries, and he wants to see you. Maybe you can borrow some skis and boots for him and teach him how to cross-country ski. I hear you've become very good at it lately."

Elizabeth blushed. Was her father referring to her skiing trips to the graveyard, or was he seriously paying her a compliment? She decided she wouldn't ask exactly what he meant.

"Okay. I am hungry. And Dad. . . ."

"Yes?"

"I'm really sorry you've been worried. I'd like to explain it all to you sometime, if you'd listen."

"I'll be glad to listen, anytime you want to talk about it." Mike Connell paused for a moment. "Elizabeth, there's a story I should tell you, about myself when I was your age. There was an old woman who sat on our family's front porch and told me of how it had been when she was young and lived in that very house."

"Grandma?" Elizabeth asked.

"No, dear. Not great-grandma, either. You see, no one but me could see her or hear her. She wasn't supposed to exist!"

"Really, Dad? Or are you making up a story to help me feel better?"

"I saw what I saw, Elizabeth, but looking back on it I'm not sure if she was real. At the time she seemed real, very real, to me. I'll tell you all about it and you can decide. And you tell me about your Steve, okay?"

They smiled at each other. "Elizabeth? I've ... I've never told your mother about my phantom old woman. Let's keep it that way, shall we?"

"Sure, Dad, sure!" This time their smiles were more like conspiratorial grins.

Chapter 21

Christmas in Wells. It was a strange time, yet a very good one as well. Elizabeth's brother, Brian, had one of the best Christmases ever, or so he said. Elizabeth found skis and boots for him, and he took to the sport naturally. "I've got hockey ankles, strong ones. That's why I'm so good at skiing," he announced. Elizabeth grinned at her younger brother's lack of modesty.

She was amazed at how quickly Brian found a group of friends his own age. There seemed to be dozens of twelve-year-olds hanging around the restaurant or the trailer, and Brian was seldom alone.

We really are quite different people, she thought. *I wonder what Brian would see in the Barkerville graveyard!*

Christmas dinner was served in the restaurant. "Oh Joan," sighed the Judge after the meal. "Do you have to leave? I don't think the MacDonalds will ever find a cook as good as you."

"You'll manage, Evan," smiled Joan Connell. "It looks

to me as if you've put on weight in the last little while. You could do with a change of cooks."

Turkey with cranberry sauce, gifts and a floor littered with wrapping paper, laughter and friends, and the deep white snow that turned the outdoors into a picture post-card — that was Christmas. Oddly enough, Elizabeth felt happy most of the time. She made no attempt to go to the graveyard, but went skiing with Brian and spent hours talking with her Dad instead. The Barkerville of 1870 — and Steve — seemed far away and unimportant now that her family was together again. Her mother, too, was more cheerful and had never mentioned Elizabeth's late-night escapade.

Everything was going smoothly, everything was comfortable and secure. Except, in one small corner of her mind, Elizabeth still thought about Steve. Even with the bustle of Christmas, the excitement of having her father and Brian with her again, and the relief of not having to deal with her mother's anger, Elizabeth worried about Steve. He had been so sick when she left him. She had promised to return on Sunday; she would have to go back to tell him that she was leaving Wells. She would miss Steve very much, but, as her father had said, she had no choice in the matter. She *had* to go back to Vancouver.

Mike and Brian Connell left for Vancouver on Saturday, the day after Boxing Day, in the station wagon. Elizabeth and her mother would take the evening flight out of Quesnel the next day. Mike Connell packed the car full, then struggled to get both Elizabeth's bike and her skis securely strapped to the top. "How you two women ever managed to acquire so much junk in just six months I'll never know." He laughed. "Elizabeth, you've got a whole library of books here. Couldn't you consider leaving some of them in Wells?" Eventually the car was packed and they were off, waving and shouting out the window. "See you Sunday. Take care. Don't miss that plane!" Then they were gone.

Elizabeth knew that she would spend only one more night in Wells before it was all over — her loneliness, the time change, Steve. Only one more night and one more day. She looked down the highway, remembering the hot, dry July day when she and her mother first came along that dusty road into Wells. So much had happened to her in six months. Now it was over, and she was going home.

She sighed deeply and turned to go into the restaurant. *I think I'm glad,* she thought. *I think I'm glad that it's over. I'll miss Steve, but it's been such a confusing time. I almost don't want to see him again. I just want to be normal and not have to think about time changes and wonder if I'm going crazy. I want to go home and forget all about the cemetery in Barkerville. I almost want to forget Steve, too. It's as if I no longer believe he exists.* She shrugged, ashamed of herself for her thoughts, and went into the hotel.

Chapter 22

The next day, Sunday, Joan Connell worked her last shift at the Jack O' Clubs Restaurant. As she left to go to work, she looked strangely at Elizabeth. "You won't. . . .I mean, I don't think it would be a good idea to go to. . . . We do have a plane to catch tonight, you know."

Elizabeth knew what her mother was trying to say. "It's okay, Mom. I'll be on that plane. Just go to work and don't worry. I'm going to visit the Judge. Besides, my skis are in Vancouver by now, aren't they? How could I go anywhere?"

Her mother looked relieved. "It's not that I don't trust you, Elizabeth, but I do think that some things should be forgotten, and the sooner the better. Have a good visit with Evan. Remind him to pick us up right at five or we'll never make it into Quesnel in time for the plane. And make sure you're all packed."

"Yes, Mom. I will." They smiled at each other with the nervous smiles of people who can't talk about what's really on their minds. "Mom?"

"Yes, Elizabeth?"

"I'm glad we're going home. I really am. Thank you."

Joan Connell put her arms around her daughter. "I'm happy you feel that way. I know it will be the best thing for you. And for me, too, Elizabeth. I'm ready to go back. I've learned a lot about myself as a person these past months, but now I want to go home, to Brian and your father and my old life."

"I know, Mom. I'll be packed and I'll make sure that the trailer is clean for the new cook. Go to work now. You don't want to be late for your last day."

"I was expecting you, Bess." The Judge opened the door to his little cabin and let her in. A fire crackled in the big iron cook stove that he used for both heat and cooking, and the cabin was warm and comfortable. "Come in, Your Majesty. Come in for a while."

Elizabeth sat nervously on the edge of the large old sofa. The Judge offered her a Coke. She drank it quickly, then gathered her courage and spoke to him. "Judge, I have to ask you a favour. You sort of believe in my time change and Steve and everything, don't you?"

"I don't know, Bess. Even after seeing you materialize in front of me in the graveyard the other evening, I still find it hard to believe. Maybe you had fallen asleep, and I didn't notice you until you stood up. Let's just say that I believe you've had some sort of *unusual* experience."

"Listen to me for a moment, Judge, please. I have to go back to the graveyard today. I promised Steve that I would. He was so sick when I left him. I *have* to see him once more. To say goodbye and... and also to prove to myself that he really exists, that I haven't just been imagining things. When Dad and Brian were here, Steve and the time change seemed so unreal. I'm confused, Judge. I have to go back once more."

"You've begun to doubt yourself, Bess. I don't know if

it's a good thing for you or not."

"I have to go to the graveyard, Judge. I have to! I promised. I can't get there by myself. Dad took my skis to Vancouver and it's too cold to walk. Please will you drive me there and wait for me? Please? I won't be long, I prommise.

"Oh, Bess. What will your mother say? I can't help you break a promise to her."

"She didn't make me promise not to go there today. Well, she sort of talked about it, but she didn't tell me not to go. Really. And we don't have to say anything to her. She's at work. She won't know. Please, Judge? It's very important to me, and she won't have to know. It's my last chance before we leave."

Evan Ryerson looked at her, one hand gently twirling the upswept corner of his moustache. "It's cold today," he announced. "I plugged in my car an hour ago. It's all warm and ready to go."

"Judge! You knew I was going to ask you to take me to the graveyard, didn't you?"

"Didn't know for certain, my dear, but I had a feeling that you couldn't leave Wells without saying all your goodbyes. And, whatever happened to you in the graveyard, that's one place I was sure you would want to say goodbye to."

"Thank you, Judge. Thank you for understanding."

"Oh, I don't understand, Bess. I wish I did. I just know that there are some things that people have to do, no matter what the consequences. I knew you would want to see your Steve once more — whoever or whatever he may be." He picked up his jacket. "Well? Shall we go?"

Elizabeth climbed the trail to the graveyard by herself. The Judge had offered to wait in the car. "Nothing happened the last time I went with you," he said. "Besides, the car is warm and it's cold out there. Don't be long, now. You have a plane to catch in a few hours."

She stood by the unknown grave, one hand resting on

the trunk of the big pine tree that shaded it. The chickadees seemed to have been discouraged by the colder weather; not one of them could be seen or heard in the graveyard. *The last time*, she thought. *The last time. I hope Steve is here. I hope he's better.*

She turned the ring. Nothing happened. She turned it again. Still, the familiar sensations of the time change failed to occur.

"Steve?" she called. "Steve, I'm here. Help me find you."

She turned the ring again and again. A few flakes of snow settled on her face — nothing else moved. The tree, the isolated grave, the ancient, anonymous headstone all stayed the same. There was no mist, no stomach wrenching, no headache. Absolutely nothing.

"Steve!" she called again. "Steve! I'm trying, I'm trying!"

She waited for a while, turning the ring often, watching in vain for the years to fall away and the new graves of 1870 to appear. But the graveyard remained unchanged — firmly entrenched in 1980. She waited and watched for a long time. Then she started down the trail.

Chapter 23

It was August, and it was hot. Barkerville lay under a cloud of dust stirred up by a busy tourist feet. The Wake-Up Jake was doing a big business in iced tea and Cokes, and the actors at the Theatre Royal sweated under their grease paint.

Elizabeth stood by her special spot in the graveyard. She leaned against the pine tree, and looked around. Small dust motes danced in the streams of sunlight that found their way between the branches of the trees, dappling the thick grass and moss with spots of gold. In the distance she could hear the sounds of horses as the Barnard's Express wagon, full of excited children, rattled along the trail. A young couple were leaving the graveyard. Thinking themselves alone, they stopped by the gate for a kiss, then, holding hands and laughing, started down the trail.

The graveyard was empty. Elizabeth stood and looked at the ring on her finger. It was still there, fitting snugly. She had worn it for a whole year — since she found it last August. *What will happen if I turn it around on my finger!* she thought. Then she laughed.

Nothing. Nothing would happen, the same way nothing had happened that December day, her final day in Wells.

Nothing. It had all been *nothing*. Steve didn't exist, had never existed, except in some strange corner of her lonely mind. Seven months away from Barkerville had convinced her that the psychiatrist, Dr. Fendell, had been right. She had found a ring and made up an incredible story around it. She had conjured up a friend for herself, a friend — or perhaps a father figure — who was truly hers because only she could see him. Well, she still had the ring. It was real — there was no doubt about that.

She was almost embarrassed to think of her experiences last winter. What had she done, all those long hours in the graveyard when she imagined she was talking to Steve? Had she slept, or daydreamed, or had she been talking to herself out loud? And what about that long, cold night that she had thought she was sitting by Steve's bedside, back in old Barkerville? She could still remember the date. It had been December 21 that Sunday, and she hadn't returned to Wells until the early hours of the next day. What had she really done for all those hours? She had actually believed she was invisible! She must have been very sick indeed.

And yet. . . . Sometimes she heard a voice or caught a glimpse of someone who reminded her of Steve, and suddenly she could see him so clearly. The slightly bent nose, the green eyes that grew greener when he was serious. The freckles. Sometimes, too, she would wake in the middle of the night, feeling his arms around her, his lips on hers, hearing his voice. "I love you, Bess. I love you."

She shook her head. That had been nonsense, and she had gotten over it. Back in the big high school, back with her friends, back in the centre of her family, she had been able to think about it, think clearly. Steve had only existed in her imagination — she was sure of that now.

She had made him up, invented him, and she shouldn't feel any sense of loss now that she realized the truth.

But she did feel a sense of loss. As if something had gone out of her life, something precious and very special. Almost as if she were no longer a whole person, but a broken half of something that had once existed.

Margaret Elizabeth Connell, snap out of it! she told herself. *Get out of here and go back and find your family. Dad said we had to leave by three in order to be in Prince George this evening.*

She was looking forward to the holiday, the first one her father had found time for in several years. They were going to the Queen Charlotte Islands for a ten day camping trip and Elizabeth had been busy reading about the islands for weeks now. The Connells had only stopped in Barkerville for the day. Elizabeth had watched the Judge give his performance, and the rest of her family were now in the Theatre Royal, deep in the plots and counter plots of this season's melodrama.

She had not gone to the Theatre Royal, choosing instead to spend some time here in the graveyard. Although she thought that she was truly over the whole experience, something made her want to come back, just one more time.

To prove to myself that I'm over it, she thought. *To show the lonely Elizabeth of last year that she is grown up, that she is sixteen now, and she can accept the fact that she was a little bit crazy for a while.*

She smiled and ran her hands through her hair, now cropped short and lying neatly about her ears. She thought of Chris, so unlike Steve. He was short, wore thick glasses and was an avid science fiction reader. They had met in the library, begun talking, and now they saw each other regularly. It was good having someone with whom she could share her interest in reading.

Chris had taken her to all the science fiction movies in town over the last few months, and last Saturday he had solemnly put aside his glasses and kissed her. Her first kiss. Well, except for Steve. It was odd how clear the memory was of the first time Steve had kissed her, clearer even than last Saturday night with Chris. *Let's face it,* she thought. *It's strange how real that whole experience was. I can shut my eyes and almost see the old graveyard and the treeless hills and . . . and Steve.*

She reached a decision. Although she knew that turning the ring was nonsense, she would try it. Nothing would happen, especially now that she no longer believed in it. But she would try it anyway, just to prove to herself that she had imagined the whole thing.

Slowly, almost as if she were performing a solemn ritual, she turned the ring around her little finger. As she had expected, nothing happened. Nothing changed. She was not back in the old Barkerville cemetery, and Steve was not there waiting for her.

She felt disappointed. *What's the matter with me! Did I really want it to happen again! I'd start thinking I'm crazy once more. I'm glad nothing happened. I'm glad! There never was a Steven Baker.*

She bent down to pat the lonely tombstone, part of the ritual she had set for herself last summer. Someone had made an attempt to clean up the wooden marker. Much of the thick moss had been scraped away exposing the lettering.

I wonder if I can read what it says now, she thought, and squatted down to see it better.

For a minute she thought she was going to faint. Her heart began to pound and tears sprang suddenly into her eyes. "It can't be, it can't be," she repeated over and over as her finger carefully traced the words now visible on the old marker.

"Steven Baker," she read. "Born August 31, 1853. Died December 22, 1870. Rest in Peace."

"Steve?" she said. "Steve. . . ."

Afterword

Although modern Barkerville and Wells have changed slightly since this was written, the Barkerville of 1870 and its characters, with the exception of Steven Baker and his family, are historically accurate. Elizabeth and the other characters from 1980 are my own invention, except for Evan Ryerson, the Judge. He is based loosely on the actor, Peter Burgis, who is the current Judge Begbie in Barkerville during the summer months.